FIRST NAMES

A-Z GUIDE TO OVER 2000 NAMES

This edition published 1993 by
Diamond Books
77-85 Fulham Palace Road
Hammersmith
London W6 8JB

Printed and bound in Great Britain

FOREWORD

Interest in names is peculiarly widespread. They are a by-product of human activity as important to the hopeful parent and the enquiring child as to the philologist or historian. In the scope of this work we have tried to include those names which have been prominent in the modern cultural development of Britain. We have made no attempt to capture all the individual variations and inventions that have occurred, especially recently, as these are far too numerous and, except in rare cases, do not have a wide application. We provide a guide to the pronunciation of the names, and describe briefly the history and development of each one. Etymologies have been kept simple; we use 'Old German' to describe both Old High and Middle High German, and we use 'Welsh' and 'Irish' so that 'Gaelic' refers to Scottish Gaelic. Occasionally the term 'Celtic' indicates a lack of evidence about which branch of that language a name first developed in. The short sketches on each main entry show how names were affected by social and political events, by literature, and by the influence of outstanding personalities, and how, in their turn, they reflect the beliefs and aspirations of English-speaking peoples. The first edition was compiled by Sandra Bance BA Hons, Mary Laird and Charles Wacher, under the supervision of Mr A.G. Hepburn ALA, former Head Librarian of the Mitchell Library, Glasgow, and Mr R. E. Adams BA ALA, of the National Library of Scotland, Edinburgh. The revised edition has been prepared by Julia Cresswell. Since the book was first compiled, there have been considerable changes in the fashion for first names. Different names are now popular, and the number of names in general use has increased. There is a much wider range in forms and spellings of these names, and great stress is put on individuality. As many of these as can be fitted in have been included, and most names in regular use can be found

PRONUNCIATION

ā as in mate   a as in pat
ē as in mete   e as in pet
ī as in mite   i as in pit
ō as in mote   o as in pot
ū as in mute   u as in nut

à as in father   th as in thin
e̱ as in her   TH as in thine
o͞o as in boot   zh as in leisure
oo as in foot   ch as in church
ow as in owl   H as in loch

The symbol ' follows stressed syllables

A

AARON m. (e'ren)

possibly from the Hebrew for 'mountaineer', or an Egyptian name of obscure meaning. It is connected with the Arabic names **Harun** and **Haroun**. In the Old Testament Aaron was the brother of Moses and first High Priest of Israel. The name has been in use since the Reformation, and has recently become more popular.

ABAGAIL, ABB(E)Y, ABBIE see ABIGAIL

ABE, ABIE see ABEL, ABRAHAM

ABEL m. (ābel)

from the Hebrew, the word may be connected with that for 'breath' or for 'son'. In the Old Testament Abel was the second son of Adam and Eve, murdered by his brother Cain. The name has been in use in England since before the Norman Conquest, and is still found occasionally. The short forms include **Abe**, **Abie** and **Nab**.

ABIGAIL *f. (ab'igāl)*

from the Hebrew, meaning 'father rejoiced'. It was the name of one of King David's wives and was much used in England during the 16th and 17th centuries, when many Old Testament names were popular. It degenerated into a term for a lady's maid and declined, but is now being revived. It is sometimes spelt **Abagail**, or **Abigal**. The short forms include **Abbie**, **Abbey**, **Abby** and GAIL.

ABNER *m. (ab'ne)*

from the Hebrew words for 'father' and 'light'. It was the name of Saul's cousin, who was also commander of Saul's army. In England, it came into use after the Reformation, and it is still found occasionally in North America.

ABRAHAM *m. (āb'reham)*

This is the name of the Old Testament patriarch, which was changed from the form **Abram**, 'high father', to Abraham, 'father of many'. It was used in England regularly after the Reformation and became popular in North America. There the abbreviation **Abe**, as in President Abe Lincoln (1809-65), was widely used. Other short forms are **Abie**, **Ham**, **Bram**

and **Braham**. Bram and Braham are sometimes used as names in their own right.

ADA *f.* (*ā̱de*)

Sometimes used as a pet form for ADELAIDE
and ADELINE, this is also a name in its own
right, possibly derived from the Old German
Eda or **Etta**, meaning 'happy'. It was fashionable in Britain in the late 18th and 19th
centuries.

ADAH *f.* (*ā'de̱*)

This name is often confused with ADA but is in
fact derived from the Hebrew word for
'ornament'. It occurs in the Old Testament
book of Genesis and is one of the oldest names
still in use. It was popular in England in the
19th century and is still used occasionally in
North America.

ADAIR *m.* (*eder'*)

This is an old Scottish name derived from the
Gaelic meaning 'of the oak tree ford'. It is still
in use, both as a first name and surname, but
is not common.

ADAM m. (ad'em)

from the Hebrew, meaning 'red', possibly refer-
ring either to the skin colour, or to the earth
from which God formed the first man, in the
Old Testament. The name was adopted by the
Irish as early as the 7th century, when St
Adamnan, 'Adam the Little', was Abbot of
Iona. It was very common in the 13th century,
and has been used ever since, particularly in
Scotland. Since the 1960s it has been increasingly popular. **Adamina** is a rare feminine
form.

ADELA f. (adāl'e)

from the Old German, meaning 'noble'. It was
common among the Normans, who brought it
to England. One of William the Conqueror's
daughters had this name. It died out but later
became fashionable among the Victorians,
sometimes in the French form **Adèle** which is
still regularly used.

ADELAIDE f. (ad'elād)

derived from Old German words meaning
'noble' and 'kind'. It was common for centuries
on the Continent but came to Britain in 1830
when Adelaide of Saxe-Coburg became queen.

Adelaide, capital city of South Australia, was named after this popular queen. ADA is sometimes used as a pet form.

ADÈLE *see* **ADELA**

ADELICE, ADELISE *see* **ALICE**

ADELINE *f.* *(ad'elēn, ad'elīn)*

Like ADELAIDE this name is derived from the Old German for 'noble'. It was first cited in England in Domesday Book, and was common during the Middle Ages. After that it disappeared until the Victorian Gothic revival. It is best known from the song *Sweet Adeline*. ADA is sometimes used as a pet form (*see also* ALINE).

ADLAI *m.* *(ad'li)*

from the Hebrew, meaning 'ornament'. The name is best known from the American politician Adlai Stevenson (1900-65).

ADRIAN *m.* **ADRIENNE** *f.(ā'drien, adrēen')*

from the Latin, meaning 'man from Adria', and the name of the Roman Emperor **Hadrian**, who built the wall across northern England. It has been used from Roman times;

a St Adrian was martyred in the 4th century and another helped organize the English Church in the 7th century. It was common from the 12th century, perhaps on account of the English Pope Adrian IV, and has become popular again recently. **Adriana** is a rare feminine form, the French **Adrienne** being more popular today. **Adrianne** is also found.

AEGIDIUS *see* GILES

AEMILIANUS *see* EMLYN

AEMILIUS *see* EMILY

AENEAS *m.* (*ēnē′es*)

the name of the legendary hero of Virgil's *Aeneid*, who is said to have escaped from the Sack of Troy to Italy, and laid the first foundations of the civilization of Rome. The name has been given in Britain since the Renaissance, but has never been common, although in Scotland it has been used to transliterate the Gaelic **Aonghus** (*see* ANGUS). ENA can be used as a feminine form.

AFRA *see* APHRA

AGATHA *f.* (*ag'ethe*)

from the Greek, meaning 'good woman', the name of a 3rd-century martyr and saint. The name was popular during the Middle Ages in various forms, including the French **Agace** and the Latin **Agacia**. It is best known as the name of the detective story writer Agatha Christie (1890-1976). The short form is **Aggie**.

AGNES *f.* (*ag'nis*)

from the Greek word meaning 'pure'. There was an early Christian martyr called Agnes, and the name was very popular from the 12th to 16th centuries in England. It had many forms, including **Annis**, **Annice**, **Annes** and **Agneta**. **Inez** is the anglicized form of the Spanish **Inés**. Agnes has always been popular in Scotland with its diminutives **Nessie** and **Nessa**. In Wales it becomes **Nest** and **Nesta**. **Aggie** is a short form shared with Agatha (*see* INA).

AIDAN *m.* (*ā'den*)

from the diminutive form of the Irish word for 'fire'. It was the name of a 7th-century Irish monk of Lindisfarne in Northumbria and enjoyed a revival during the 19th century and

15

is still used. **Hayden (Haydon, Haydn)** is said to be a Welsh form of the name.

AILEEN *f.* (*ālēn*)

from the Irish form of **Helen**. It is popular in the British Isles today, especially in Scotland and Ireland. (*see* EILEEN).

AILSA *f.* (*āl'se*)

the name of the Scottish island Ailsa Craig, used as a first name. It has now spread from Scotland to the rest of the country.

AIMÉ *see* ESMÉ

AIMÉE *see* AMY

AINE *see* AITHNE

AINSLEY *m. and f.* (*āns'li*)

a place and surname used as a first name. It comes from Old English and probably means 'Agen's meadow'. It is also spelt **Ainslie**.

AIR *see* ERIC

AISHA *see* AYESHA

AITHNE f. (eth'ni)

from the Irish, meaning 'little fire', it has been popular for centuries in Ireland. In legend **Aine** is queen of the fairies in south Munster. As a result of the revival of Celtic names it is coming back into use in Scotland and Ireland. Modern variants include **Ethne** and **Eithne**.

ALAN m., **ALANA** f. (al'en, alan'e, alān'e)

probably from an old British word meaning 'harmony'. It has appeared in various forms from early times. In England it first became popular after the Norman Conquest as **Alain** and **Alein**, the French forms. These developed into Alleyne which is preserved as a surname. Alan, **Allan, Allen** and **Alun** are in use today. Alana, the feminine form, is also spelt **Allana**, **Alanah** and **Alanna**. The actress **Lana** Turner made the short form well known.

ALASDAIR, ALASTAIR,
see **ALEXANDER**

ALBAN m. (awl'ben)

from the Latin Albanus, meaning 'man from Alba', and the name of the first British martyr. Various legends give the town of St Albans as the birthplace and the place of execution of this saint. The name was never common, but it was revived under the influence of the Oxford Movement in the 19th century. **Albin** and **Albinus** are variants which appear occasionally.

ALBERIC, ALBERY *see* AUBREY

ALBERT *m. (al'bet)*

from the Old German words meaning 'noble' and 'bright'. The Old English form was ETHLE-BERT, famous for the Kentish king who welcomed St Augustine. This was replaced after the conquest by the French **Aubert**. **Halbert** was a northern English variant. Albert became very popular after the marriage of Queen Victoria to Prince Albert of Saxe-Coburg. The feminine forms **Alberta** and **Albertine** are rare. **Bert** and **Bertie** are short forms.

ALBIN, ALBINUS *see* ALBAN

ALBINA *f. (albēne)*

from the Latin, meaning 'white'. The name was often used in the 17th and 18th centuries, but is rarely found today. The Italian form

Albinia was introduced into England by the Cecil family and has been used by them since.

ALDOUS m. (*awl′dus*)

from the Old German Aldo, meaning 'old'. It has been used in the eastern counties of England since the 13th century and has given rise to various surnames like **Aldhouse** and **Aldiss**. **Aldo** is still in use in North America. The writer Aldous Huxley (1894-1963) is a famous modern British example.

ALEC see ALEXANDER

ALED m. (*a′led*)

a Welsh river, best known as the name of the singer Aled Jones. There is a feminine form **Aledwen**. It means 'offspring, young one'.

ALEIN see ALAN

ALESSANDRA see SANDRA

ALETHEA f. (*alē′thēe*)

from the Greek word meaning 'truth'. It was much used in the 17th century in England. Variant forms include **Alethia** and **Aletia**.

ALEXANDER *m.* (*alekzàn'de*)

from the Greek word meaning 'defender of
men'. It was made famous in the 4th century
BC by Alexander the Great, and was very
popular in England in the Middle Ages,
appearing often in the French form
Alysaundre. In Scotland it has been widely
used both in the English form and the Gaelic
variants **Alasdair, Alastair, Alistair** and
Alister, with the pronunciation (*a'lister*).
Sandy is a common pet form. Short forms are
Alex, Alec and **Lex**.

ALEXANDRA *f.* (*alekzàn'dre*)

feminine form of ALEXANDER. It was in use in
England by the 13th century, but only became
popular with the marriage of the Prince of
Wales (later King Edward VII) to Princess
Alexandra of Denmark. SANDRA was originally
the Italian diminutive form, but has become
established as a name in its own right. It
shares pet and short forms with ALEXANDER.
Alexandria and **Alexandrina** are also found.

ALEXIS *m. and f.* (*alek'sis*)

from the Greek, meaning 'helper' or 'defender'.
The name is common in Russia and has been

used occasionally in the 20th century in Britain and North America for both boys and girls, although it is more common for girls. It is now strongly associated with the character played by Joan Collins in the television series *Dynasty*. **Alexie** and, for girls, **Alexia** are also used.

ALF, ALFIE *see* ALFRED

ALFRED *m.* (al'fred)

from two Old English words, meaning 'elf' (hence 'good') and 'counsel'. It is also a possible development of the name **Ealdfrith**, meaning 'old peace', and was the name of a 7th-century king of Northumbria, sometimes being written **Alfrid**. When its spelling was latinized, the name developed into **Alured** and then into **Avery**, which survives as a surname. The original Alfred was reintroduced in the 18th century and became very popular in the 19th. **Alf, Alfie** and **Fred** are diminutives and there is a feminine form **Alfreda**.

ALGERNON *m.* (al'jenon)

from the Norman French nickname meaning 'with whiskers'. It was uncommon from Tudor times up to the 19th century when its use became general, although it is rarely used today. The usual diminutives are **Algie** or **Algy**.

ALIA *see* ELLA

ALICE *f.* (*al'is*)

from the Old German word for 'nobility'. It originally had the form **Adelice** or **Adelise**. A number of variants remained popular from the Middle Ages until the 17th century, when it declined in favour. It was revived again in the 19th century together with the variant **Alicia**, and achieved immortality in Lewis Carroll's *Alice in Wonderland*. **Alison** is a variant which became popularly established at the same time as Alice, especially in Scotland. **Alys** is the Welsh form. **Ali, Allie** and **Alley** are used as pet forms, and the name is sometimes spelt **Allice, Allyce** and **Alyssa**.

ALINE *f.* (*à'lēn, a'lēn*)

originally a short form of ADELINE but now definitely established as an independent name, much more popular than the declining Adeline. Variant forms are **Arleen** and **Arline**.

ALISON f. (al'is<u>e</u>n)

originally a diminutive of ALICE adopted in the 13th century, but soon treated as a separate name. It has remained popular since, especially in Scotland. Pet forms include **Ally**, **Ailie** and ELSIE.

ALISTAIR, ALISTER see ALEXANDER

ALLAN, ALLEN, ALLEYNE see ALAN

ALLEGRA f. (aleg're)

An Italian word meaning 'cheerful, lively', given by the poet Lord Byron to his daughter and still used occasionally as a result.

ALLY, AILIE see ALISON

ALMA f. (al'm<u>e</u>)

There are many opinions about the derivation of this name. It possibly had its origin in the Hebrew word for 'maiden', the Latin for 'kind' or the Italian for 'soul'. The name became very popular after the battle of Alma in the Crimean War, and is still found occasionally.

ALOYSIUS *m. (alōish'es)*

This is a latinization of **Aloys**, an old Provencal form of LOUIS. There was a popular Spanish saint of this name in the 16th century and Roman Catholics continue to use the name in this country.

ALTHEA *f. (al'thēe)*

from the Greek for 'wholesome'. It appears to have been introduced to England with various other classical names during the Stuart period, and appeared in the charming lyric by Richard Lovelace *To Althea from Prison*.

ALUN *see* ALAN

ALURED *see* ALFRED

ALVIN *m. (al'vin)*

from the Old English **Alwine**, meaning either 'friend of all' or 'noble friend'. This is not common in Britain, but is still found fairly frequently in North America. **Aylwin** is an alternative form of the name.

ALYS *see* ALICE

ALYSAUNDRE *see* ALEXANDER

AMABEL *f. (am'ebel)*

from the Latin for 'lovable'. It has been in use in England in various forms since the 12th century. The short form MABEL early became established as an independent name.

AMANDA *f. (eman'de)*

from the Latin, meaning 'lovable'. It appears first in Restoration plays, where many names from classical sources were introduced or fabricated. It has remained in use since and is still popular. **Mandy** is a pet form also used as a name in its own right.

AMARYLLIS *f. (ameril'is)*

originally from Greek, probably meaning 'fresh stream', and used by Greek poets as a name for pastoral heroines. It served the same purpose for Latin poets, and was introduced into English poetry in the 17th century.

AMATA *see* AMY

AMBER *f. (ami'be)*

The jewel, used as a first name. It was not used before this century.

AMBROSE m. (am'brōz)

from the Greek for 'divine'. There was a 4th-century St Ambrose who was Bishop of Milan and exerted a strong influence in the West Country. The name is found in Domesday Book and has been used occasionally since. The Welsh name **Emrys** is derived from Ambrosius Aurelianus, the 5th-century leader of the Celts against the Saxons. There is a rare feminine form **Ambrosine**.

AMELIA f. (emē'lie)

from an Old German word possibly meaning 'labour', and the root of many German names. Another influence on the name's development is the Roman family name Amelius. It was introduced into Britain under the Hanoverian royal line and was often anglicized to EMILY, as in the case of George III's youngest daughter, Princes Emily. The short form is usually **Milly**.

AMINTA, AMYNTA see ARAMINTA

AMOS m. (ā'mos)

from the Hebrew for 'strong'. It was the name of an Old Testament prophet and was adopted by the Puritans after the Reformation in

England, when saints' names were in disfavour. Since then it has become more common in North America.

AMY f. (ā'mi)

from the French, meaning 'beloved woman'. There was a 13th-century saint with the Latin form of the name, **Amata**, who made it fairly popular, especially among Roman Catholics. In the 19th century, Sir Walter Scott's novel *Kenilworth*, about Amy Robsart, the tragic wife of the Earl of Leicester, made the name fashionable, and it is well known in Britain today. A famous 20th-century holder of the name was Amy Johnson, the pioneer flyer. **Aimée** is the French original of this name (*see* ESMÉ).

ANASTASIA f. (anestà'zie, anestāz'ie)

from the Greek, meaning 'resurrection', and the name of a 4th-century saint and martyr. It became fashionable in England in the 13th century, though it was usually abbreviated to **Anstey** or **Anstice**, which survive today as surnames. It has always been very popular in Russia, and a daughter of the last Tsar of Russia, called Anastasia, is said to have escaped from the execution in which the rest

27

of her family died, in 1918. Several books, plays and films have been written about her, and they have made the name better known in Britain in the 20th century. STACEY is a North American pet form.

ANDREW *m.*, ANDREA *f.* (*an'dróò, an'drāe*)

from the Greek for 'manly'. Andrew is the name of the Apostle who is patron saint of Scotland and Russia, and first appears in England in Domesday Book. It has been used in Britain continuously, and has enjoyed particular favour in Scotland. It was chosen by Queen Elizabeth II and I for her second son, in 1960, and is one of the commonest boys' names in Britain today. The diminutives include **Andy, Dandy** (Scots) and **Drew**. The Italian form, **Andrea**, is used for the girl's name. The French form, **André**, is sometimes used for boys.

ANEURIN *m.* (*enoi'rin*)

possibly the Welsh form of Latin **Honorius**, meaning 'honourable', or a compound of the Welsh words for 'all' and 'gold', with a diminutive ending. It also appears in the form **Aneirin**. It has always been popular in Wales, with its diminutive **Nye** which became familiar as the name of Labour politician Aneurin Bevan (1897-1960).

ANGELA f. (an'jele)

from the Latin *angelus*, originally derived from the Greek word meaning 'messenger'. In England it was used regularly as a girl's name, side by side with the masculine form **Angel**, until it was barred as impious by the Puritans. **Angelica** enjoyed favour in literary contexts between the 15th and 16th centuries. Angela was revived in the 19th century together with **Angeline** and **Angelina**. **Angelique** is the French form.

ANGHARAD f. (an'heràd)

A Welsh name meaning 'much loved'. The actress Angharad Rees has made the name more widely known.

ANGUS m. (an'ges)

from the Gaelic **Aonghus**, meaning 'one choice'. It appears in Irish legend and early Celtic church history, and became firmly established in Scotland. The name became associated with the classical myth of AENEAS in the 15th century, and this form was also used.

ANN *f. (an)*

from the Hebrew HANNAH, meaning 'grace'. Hannah, the name of the mother of the prophet Samuel in the Old Testament, has been in use in England since the Reformation, and was very popular in North America. The French form **Anne** was introduced into Britain in the 13th century and the name has enjoyed great popularity since, being the name of six queens and now of the only daughter of Queen Elizabeth II and I. Diminutives include **Nan, Nanette, Nanny,** NANCY and **Annie,** as well as the variants **Anita, Annette** and **Anona.** Ann has often formed part of compounds such as Mary Ann (which became MARIAN or Marianne), Carol Anne, Joy Anne, etc. Another form, **Anna,** is very often used. **Anneka** is a Dutch pet form, and **Anya** is from the Spanish pronunciation of the name.

ANNA *see* ANN, HANNAH

ANNABEL(LA) *f. (an'ebel(e))*

possibly from the Latin *amabilis*, meaning 'lovable', as a variant of AMABEL. Its use in

Scotland is recorded before that of **Ann**, though it is now sometimes thought of as a compound of Anna and the latin *bella*, meaning 'beautiful'. Diminutives include **Bel, Belle** and **Bella**.

ANNE, ANNETTE, ANNIE see **ANN**

ANNES see **AGNES**

ANNIS, ANNICE see **AGNES**

ANNORA see **HONOR**

ANONA see **ANN**

ANTHEA f. (an'thie)

from the Greek *antheos*, meaning 'flowery'. This name seems to have been introduced by the pastoral poets of the 17th century and it has been in use ever since, although not until the 20th century was it very widely known.

ANTOINETTE see **ANTONY**

ANT(H)ONY *m.*, **ANTONIA** (*an'teni, antō'nēs*)

from the name of a Roman clan. Its most famous member was Marcus Antonius, the Mark Antony of Shakespeare's *Julius Caesar* and *Antony and Cleopatra*. The name was very popular in the Middle Ages as a result of the influence of St Antony the Great and St Antony of Padua. The alternative spelling, **Anthony**, was introduced after the Renaissance, when it was assumed that the name was derived from the Greek *anthos*, meaning 'flower'. The usual form is **Tony**, which is also used for the feminine forms Antonia and **Antoinette**. A feminine short form, **Toni**, is also found, as are **Toinette**, **Net** and **Nettie**, from Antoinette. **Anton**, a Continental form of the name, has recently started to be used for boys.

ANYA *see* **ANN**

AOIFFE *see* **EVE**

AONGHUS *see* **AENEAS, ANGUS**

APHRA *f.* (*af're*)

from the Hebrew word, meaning 'dust'. It is best known from the playwright, novelist and

spy, Mrs Aphra Behn (1644-89), said to have
been the first woman in England to have
earned her living as a writer. It is also spelt
Afra.

APRIL f. (ā'pril)

from the name of the month. Like JUNE it has
been used as a girl's name in the 20th century.

ARABELLA f. (arebel'e)

a possible variant from AMABEL, though it
could be derived from the Latin for 'obliging'.
It has been widely used in Scotland in the
forms **Arabel** and **Arabella**. There was also a
rare form, **Arbell**, but this has disappeared.

ARAMINTA f. (aramint'e)

This name appears to have been made up by
Sir John Vanbrugh (1664-1726) to use in one
of his plays. It may have been influenced by
Aminta or **Amynta**, an ancient Greek name
meaning 'protector'. They share the short
forms **Minta** and **Minty**.

ARCHIBALD m. (à'chibawld)

from the Old German words meaning 'true'
and 'bold'. The Old English form was used in

East Anglia before the Norman Conquest and also appears with Norman connections in Domesday Book. Thereafter it became primarily Scottish, and was associated particularly with the Douglas and Campbell families. The most usual diminutive is **Archie**.

ARETHA *f. (arē´the)*

Aretha or **Areta** is the Greek word for virtue. It is not a usual name, but has become well known through the singer Aretha Franklin.

ARIADNE *f. (ariad´ni)*

This is a Greek name of obscure origin. In Greek mythology Ariadne was the daughter of King Minos of ancient Crete. She helped Theseus to escape from the labyrinth by giving him a 'clue' of thread to mark his way. The name has been used occasionally in Britain in the 20th century. The French and Italian forms **Ariane** and **Arianna** are also found.

ARLEEN, ARLINE *see* ALINE

ARMINEL *m. (à´minel)*

This name is probably derived from the Old German *Herman*, meaning 'soldier'. **Armin,** an English form of the French **Armand**, is found in the 17th and 18th centuries, and Arminel may be a diminutive of this. The latter seems to have been confined to the West Country where it survives to this day.

ARNOLD m. (â'neld)

from the Old German **Arnwalt**, for 'eaglepower'. It appeared in various forms, both Germanic and French, in the Middle Ages, and dropped out of use between the 17th and late 19th centuries when it had a revival.

ART see ARTHUR

ARTEMISIA f. (àtemēz'ie)

from the Greek, meaning 'belonging to Artemis'. **Artemis** was the Greek goddess of wild animals, vegetation, childbirth and the hunt, comparable to Roman Diana. Artemisia was the name of the queen of Caria in the 4th century BC, who built the Mausoleum at Halicarnassus for her husband. She was also celebrated as a botanist and medical researcher. The name was first used in Britain in the 18th century and still survives in some families.

ARTHUR *m.* (*à'the*)

The origin of this name is disputed. Possible sources are the Welsh word for 'bear', the Irish word meaning 'stone', and the Roman clan name Artorius. The first mention of the British hero, King Arthur, is in the 8th-century *Historia Britonum* of Nennius. Between the 13th and 16th centuries the name was spelt **Artur**. There was a revival of the name in the 19th century when Queen Victoria's younger son was christened Arthur. **Art** is used as a short form, particularly in America.

ARUNDEL *f.* (*a'rendel*)

This is a place and surname used as a first name. It probably comes from the French word for 'a swallow'.

ASA *m.* (*ā'se*)

The Hebrew word meaning 'physician'. It is particularly associated with the North of England.

ASHLEY *m.* and *f.* (*ash'lē*)

A place and surname, meaning 'ash-field', used as a first name. It is very popular in Australia and in the United States, where its popularity may be connected with its use as a man's name in *Gone with the Wind*. It is also found as **Ashleigh**.

ASPATIA *f. (aspā'zie)*

from the Greek for 'welcome'. This name occurs in a play called *The Maid's Tragedy* by Beaumont and Fletcher, which was first performed in 1611. The name was used very occasionally thereafter.

ASTRID *f. (as'trid)*

from the Old German words meaning 'god' and 'strength'. The name of the wife of St Olaf of Norway, it has long been popular in Scandinavia, and has been used in Britain in the 20th century. Its popularity was no doubt increased by the much loved Belgian queen Astrid, who died in a motor accident in 1935.

ATHENE *f. (athēnē)*

This is the name of the Greek goddess of war and peace, and in Roman times, of wisdom. It has been used occasionally as a girl's name in Britain.

AUBERON *see* AUBREY

AUBERT *see* ALBERT

AUBREY *m. (aw'bri)*

from the Old German, meaning 'elf' and 'ruler'.
In medieval romance the diminutive **Auberon**
was used, and Shakespeare adopted it in the
variant form **Oberon**, for *A Midsummer
Night's Dream*. The German form **Alberic**
developed first into **Albery** and later into
Aubrey, which has survived as a boy's name,
though not a common one.

AUDREY *f. (aw'dri)*

the short form of **Etheldreda**, from the Old
English for 'noble' and 'strength'. It first
appears in written form in the 16th century,
and was used mostly by country folk until the
late 19th century, when it came into general
use.

AUGUSTA *f.*, AUGUSTUS *m. (awgus'te, awgus'tes)*

from the Latin for 'venerable'. Augustus was
adopted as a title by some of the German princes after the Renaissance, and was introduced

to Britain as a Christian name by the Hanoverians. **Augusta** was popular in the early 19th century. **Gus** and **Gussie** are pet forms.

AUGUSTINE, AUSTIN *m.* (*awgus'tin, os'tin*)

from a diminutive of Latin AUGUSTUS, meaning 'venerable'. The shortened form, **Austin** or **Austen**, was very popular in the Middle Ages on account of St Augustine, the first Archbishop of Canterbury. Though better known as a surname it is still used as a personal name. Augustine was revived in the 19th century by the Oxford Movement and has remained in use since (*see* AUGUSTUS). In America Augustin is pronounced (*awgustēn*).

AURELIA *f.* (*awrēlie*)

from the Latin *aurelius*, meaning 'gold'. It has been used since the 17th century, and recently a short form, **Auriol**, has appeared.

AURORA *f.* (*awraw're*)

from the Latin name of the goddess of the dawn. It was introduced into Britain at the time of the Renaissance. It has often been used in poetic contexts, as in Browning's *Aurora Leigh* (*see also* DAWN).

AUSTEN, AUSTIN *see* AUGUSTINE

AVERIL *f. and m.* (*ā'veril*)

probably from the Old English *eofor*, 'boar' and *hild*, 'battle', which appears as **Everild** in the 7th century. It was regularly in use until the 17th century, since when it has been less common. **Averell** Harriman, the American statesman, shows a variant form, which has been used as a masculine name in North America at least. The modern form Averil is often confused with AVRIL.

AVERY *see* ALFRED

AVIS *f.* (*ā'vis*)

The origin of this name, which was popular in England in the Middle Ages, is obscure. It occurred only rarely between the 16th and 19th centuries and was sometimes spelt **Avice**. It is still a rather uncommon name.

AVRIL *f.* (*av'ril*)

from the French for 'April'. The name has become popular in the 20th century, mainly for girls born in April (*see* AVERIL).

AYESHA f. (ae'she)

from the Arabic, meaning 'woman'. It was the name of the prophet Muhammad's favourite wife. In Rider Haggard's novel *She*, it is the name of 'She who must be obeyed'. It is also spelt **Aisha** and **Ayeisha**.

AYLMER see **ELMER**

AYLWIN see **ALVIN**

B

BAB, BABS *see* **BARBARA**

BABETTE *see* **ELIZABETH**

BARBARA *f.* (*bà'bre*)

from the Greek *barbaros*, meaning 'strange' or
'foreign', and associated with St Barbara, a
3rd-century martyr. The name was little used
after the Reformation, but in the 20th century
it became very popular again. Abbreviations
include **Bab** and **Babs**. The variant form **Bar-
bra** has recently become popular. **Barbie** is a
pet form.

BARNABAS *m.* (*bà'nebes*)

from the Hebrew, meaning 'son of exhortation
or consolation', and best known as the name
bestowed upon the New Testament companion
of St Paul. The diminutive, **Barnaby**, was
popular in the 19th century, when Dickens
wrote a novel called *Barnaby Rudge*. The name

is having a revival now, together with its short form, **Barney**, which it shares with Bernard.

BARNEY *see* **BARNABAS, BERNARD**

BARRY *m. (bar'i)*

from the Irish *bearach*, meaning 'spear'. For a long time it remained an exclusively Irish name, associated with an Irish saint. It is also the name of a Welsh hermit, who gave his name to Barry Island. It is now in general use.

BARTHOLOMEW *m. (bàthol'emū)*

from the Hebrew, meaning 'son of **Talmai**', surname of the Apostle Nathanael. It was very popular in the Middle Ages when the cult of St Bartholomew was at its height. St Bartholomew's hospital in London was founded in the 12th century and an annual Bartholomew Fair was held in London to provide funds for it, which was only suppressed in the 19th century. The name is still in use, with its short forms **Bart** and **Bat**.

BASIL *m. (baz'el)*

from the Greek *basileios*, meaning 'kingly'. It was probably brought to England by the

Crusaders, and it has remained in use ever since. Diminutives include **Bas** or **Baz**, and **Basie**, and there are two feminine forms, **Basilia** and **Basilie**. These were common in the Middle Ages, but are hardly ever found today.

BASTIAN, BASTIEN *see* SEBASTIAN

BAT *see* BARTHOLOMEW

BEA, BEATTY *see* BEATRICE

BEATA *f.* (bē′ta, bēä′te)

from the Latin *beatus*, meaning 'blessed' or 'happy'. Both a name in its own right and used as a pet form of BEATRICE.

BEATRICE *f.* (bē′etris)

from the Latin *beatrix*, meaning 'bringer of happiness'. It has strong literary associations. Dante's Beatrice is probably the best known, but Shakespeare also used the name in *Much Ado About Nothing*. In the form **Beatrix**, the name is remembered for the writer of Children's stories, Beatrix Potter. Short forms include **Bea, Beatty** and **Trixie**. There is also a Welsh variant, **Bettrys**.

BECKY *see* **REBECCA**

BEL *see* **BELINDA**

BEL, BELLA, BELLE *see* **ANNABEL, ISABEL**

BELINDA *f.* (*belin'de*)

from the Old German compound word, the latter part of which means 'a snake' (*see* LINDA). Its popular use began in the 18th century when it was used in plays by Congreve and Vanbrugh, and in Pope's poem *The Rape of the Lock*. Short forms include **Bel**, **Linda** and **Lindy**.

BEN, BENNY *see* **BENJAMIN**

BENEDICT *m.* (*ben'edict*)

from the Latin *benedictus*, meaning 'blessed', and most familiar as the name of St Benedict, founder of the Benedictine Order. It was common in medieval England in the forms **Bennet** and **Benedick**. The latter is the name of a character in Shakespeare's *Much Ado About Nothing*. There is a feminine form **Benedicta**, but the Spanish-American **Benita** is more common.

BENJAMIN m. (ben'jemin)

from the Hebrew, meaning 'son of the south' or 'right hand', which might imply 'son of strength'. The Old Testament story of Benjamin, son of Jacob, gave the name the added implications of a favoured, youngest son. The commonest pet forms are **Ben, Benny**, and **Benjy**.

BENNET see **BENEDICT**

BERENICE f. (berenēs')

from the Greek *Pherenice*, meaning 'bringer of victory'. It was spread by the imperial conquests of Alexander the Great over Europe and Asia. It was especially popular in Egypt, during the period of Macedonian rule, and its use spread also to the family of Herod of Judea. **Bernice** is a modern form of the name, and **Bunny** is sometimes used as a pet form.

BERNADETTE f. (benedet')

from the French diminutive of BERNARD. It has been used regularly in Britain, due to the influence of St Bernadette of Lourdes, who lived in the mid-19th century. **Bernadine** is another form of the name, and **Bernie** the short form.

BERNARD m. (be'ned)

from the Old German and Old English compound of 'bear' and 'hard', implying strength and courage. It was very popular in the Middle Ages. Two important saints having the name were St Bernard of Menthon, after whom St Bernard dogs are named, and St Bernard of Clairvaux who inspired the Second Crusade. It has remained in use ever since. The most usual short forms are **Bernie** and **Barney** (*see* BARNABAS).

BERNICE *see* BERENICE

BERRY *see* BERTRAM

BERT, BERTIE *see* ALBERT, BERTRAM, BERTRAND, GILBERT, HERBERT, HUBERT, ROBERT

BERTHA f. (ber'the)

from the Old German word *beraht*, meaning 'bright'. The first famous English Bertha was the wife of King Ethelbert of Kent who welcomed St Augustine to England. In the Middle

Ages both Bertha and **Berta** were popular, and the name has been regularly used since, although it is rather uncommon at present.

BERTRAM m. (ber'trem)

from the Old German beraht-hraban, meaning 'bright' and 'raven', the bird associated with the god Odin. The name has been used in England since the early Middle Ages, and has the diminutives **Bert** and **Bertie**, and the less common **Berry**.

BERTRAND m. (ber'trend)

the French form of BERTRAM, now used in Britain as a name in its own right. It shares the diminutives **Bert** and **Bertie** with Bertram.

BERYL f. (ber'il)

from the gem, beryl, the name of which is related to the Arabic for crystal. It did not appear before the 19th century, but has been popular in the early and middle 20th century.

BESS, BESSIE see ELIZABETH

BETH see ELIZABETH

BETHANY *f. (beth'eni)*

a girl's name taken from a New Testament place name, the village where Lazarus lived. The short form **Bethan** is used independently, and is also a pet form of ELIZABETH in Wales.

BETSY, BETTY *see* **ELIZABETH**

BETTINA *f. (bete'ne)*

an Italian pet form of ELIZABETH which was a popular given name in the 1960s.

BETTRYS *see* **BEATRICE**

BEVERL(E)Y *m. and f. (bev'eli)*

from the Old English, meaning 'of the beaver-meadow'. This name survives as a surname and Christian name both in Britain and North America.

BEVIS *m. (bev'is)*

This is a French name introduced into England by the Norman Conquest. It has been rarely used since, although a novel by Richard Jeffries called *Bevis, the Story of a Boy* (1882), may have resulted in a slight revival.

BIANCA *see* **BLANCHE**

BIDDY *see* **BRIDGET**

BILL, BILLIE *see* **WILLIAM**

BILLIE, BILLY *f.* (*bil'lē*)

This pet form of the boy's name WILLIAM is being used increasingly as a girl's name, particularly in America. The tennis player **Billie-Jean** King made one such form well known, and **Billy Joe** is another popular combination.

BLAISE *m.* (*blāz*)

from the French, meaning either one who comes from the region of Blois, or, derived from Latin, 'stammerer'. It is also spelt **Blase** and **Blaze**.

BLAKE *m. and f.* (*blāk*)

The surname, from the Old English meaning 'black, dark-complexioned', used as a first name. At the moment it is more common as a boy's name.

BLANCHE *f. (blànsh)*

This is a popular French name which was brought to England in the 13th century. It means 'white' or 'fair-skinned'. The Italian form **Bianca** was used by Shakespeare, and both are still found.

BLASE, BLAZE *see* BLAISE

BLODWEN *f. (blod'win)*

This is a Welsh name meaning 'white flower', and rarely found outside Wales.

BOB *see* ROBERT

BOBBIE, BOBBY *m. and f. (bo'be)*

These pet forms of ROBERT and ROBERTA are used as names in their own right, and in combinations such as **Bobby Joe**.

BONNIE, BONNY *m. and f. (bo'ne)*

This is very often used as a nickname but it may have its origin in the Latin *bona*, meaning 'good', which was used in the Middle Ages. It is being used increasingly as a name in its own right.

BORIS m. *(bor'is)*

from the Russian word for 'fight'. It has been used occasionally in Britain and North America in the 20th century, possibly due to cultural influences such as Moussorgsky's opera *Boris Godunov*, the film actor Boris Karloff, and lately, perhaps the author of *Dr. Zhivago*, Boris Pasternak.

BRADLEY m. *(brad'lē)*

a surname from the Old English, meaning 'wide meadow', used as a first name. **Brad(d)** is a short form.

BRAM *see* **ABRAHAM**

BRAND *see* **BRENDA**

BRANDON m. *(bran'den)*

a place and surname from the Old English, meaning 'a hill where broom grows', used as a first name.

BRANWEN f. *(bran'wen)*

from the Welsh, meaning 'beautiful raven'. This name is associated with a legend in the

Mabinogion and with the story of Tristan and Iseult. It is still in use in Wales.

BRENDA f. (bren'de)

probably a feminine form of the Norseman's name **Brand**, meaning 'a sword', found in the Shetlands and used by Walter Scott in his novel *The Pirate*. It has been used regularly since the 19th century.

BRENDAN m. (bren'den)

from the name of the 6th-century Irish saint credited in legend with the discovery of America. It is still in use today, particulary in Ireland.

BRET(T) m. (bret)

from an Old French word meaning 'a Briton' or 'a Breton'. It was given some currency in the last century by the American author Bret Harte, and is now increasingly popular.

BRIAN m. (brī'en)

a Celtic name, the origin of which is obscure, though it may be derived from words meaning 'hill' and 'strength'. It was known mainly in

Celtic areas until the Norman Conquest, when it was introduced to England. Brian Boru, sometimes spelt **Brien**, was a famous Irish King of the 11th century. The name continued to be popular in England until Tudor times, but after that it disappeared until it was reintroduced from Ireland in the 18th century. Today the spelling **Bryan** is also found.

BRIDE, BRIDIE *see* BRIDGET

BRIDGET *f.* *(brij'it)*

This may be derived either from a Celtic goddess whose name meant 'strength', from the 5th-century Irish saint, Bridget, or from a 14th-century Swedish saint Brigitto, whose name meant 'mountain protection'. The Irish name also appears in the forms **Brigid**, **Brigit**, and **Bride**, with the diminutives **Bridie** and **Biddy**. **Britt** is a pet form of the Swedish **Birgitta**.

BRISEIDA *see* CRESSIDA

BRONWEN *f.* *(bron'win)*

from the Welsh words meaning 'white breast'. This name has long been popular in Wales and is surrounded by ancient legend.

BROOKE *m. and f. (bróŏk)*

the surname, meaning 'a brook', used as a first
name. The actress Brooke Shields is a well-
known example.

BRUCE *m. (bróŏ's)*

a Scottish surname which came to Britain at
the time of the Norman Conquest. It derives
from the name of the village of Brieuse in
Normandy. A member of this family, Robert
Bruce, became King of Scotland, and was the
ancestor of the Stuart Kings. It has only been
used as a Christian name since the 19th
century, although it is now popular both in
Scotland and England. **Brucie** is a pet form.

BRUNO *m. (bróŏ'nō)*

This is a rather uncommon name from the Old
English for 'brown'. It was used in England
before the Norman Conquest, but is now
usually thought of as a German name.

BRYAN *see* BRIAN

BRYN *m. (brin)*

a Welsh name, meaning 'hill'. **Brynmor**, 'large
hill', is also used.

BRYONY f. (bri'ōni)

the climbing hedgerow plant used as a name. The word comes from ancient Greek and means 'to grow luxuriantly'.

BUCK m. (buk)

Buck was a popular term in the 18th century for a dashing or fashionably-dressed man. It is usually only used as a nickname.

BUDDY m. (bud'e)

This word for a friend is occasionally used as a first name, but is usually a nickname. The singer Buddy Holly, for example, was christened Charles.

BUNNY see **BERENICE**

BUNTY f. (bun'te)

This was a traditional name for a pet lamb, which came into use for girls after 1911, when it was used in a very successful play called *Bunty Pulls the Strings*. However, it is usually a nickname.

BURT see **BERT**

C

CADDY *see* **CAROLINE**

CADFAEL *m. (cad'val)*

a Welsh name, meaning 'battle metal', recently given publicity as the name of the hero of the novels of Ellis Peters.

CADWALLADER *m. (kadwol'ede)*

from the Welsh, meaning 'battle chief', and one of a series of names with the Welsh word for battle as the root (*see* CHAD). It is found in Wales and in North America.

CAITLIN *see* **KATHARINE**

CAIUS, GAIUS *m. (kī'us, gī'us)*

a Roman first name, meaning 'rejoice', which is still used occasionally. The Welsh name **Cai**, **Kai** or **Kay**, well known as the name of Sir

Kay, King Arthur's foster-brother, is derived from this.

CALEB m. (kā′leb)

from the Hebrew *Kalebh*, meaning 'intrepid' or 'dog'. First appearing in the 16th century, it is now usually found in North America and Scotland.

CALLIOPE f. (kaleo′pē)

the ancient Greek Muse of epic poetry, whose name meant 'beautiful face'. It is not a common name, but is sometimes found in the short form **Cally**.

CALUM, CALLUM see COLUM, MALCOLM

CALVIN m. (kal′vin)

from the surname of the 16th century French religious reformer Jean Cauvin or Chauvin, latinized to Calvinus, and adopted as a Christian name by Protestants. It may be derived from the Old French *chauve*, meaning 'bald'. It is most commonly found in North America and Scotland.

CAMERON *m.* (*kam'eren*)

from the Gaelic, meaning 'crooked nose'. It is the name of a famous Scottish clan. Its use as a Christian name has now spread from Scotland.

CAMILLA *f.* (*kemil'e*)

a Latin name, attributed by the Latin poet Virgil (1st century BC), to a queen of the Volsci tribe, and therefore possibly of Etruscan origin. It was first recorded in Britain in 1205. The 18th century novel *Camilla* by Madame D'Arblay may have increased its popularity, as may Greta Garbo's film role as *Camille*, (the French form of the name) in the 20th century. **Milly** and **Millie** can be used as short forms.

CANDICE, CANDACE *f.* (*kan'dis*)

This is an ancient title of the Queen of Ethiopia. In the past it was pronounced (*kandā'sē*). The name is also spelt **Candis**, and **Candy** is a short form.

CANDIDA *f.* (*kan'dide*)

from the Latin, meaning 'white'. It was the name of several saints, amongst them one from

Naples whom St Paul is said to have cured. The name was not used in Britain until the early 20th century and its introduction was probably effected by G.B. Shaw's play *Candida* and its heroine (*see* BLANCHE).

CANDY *see* CANDICE

CARA *f.* (*ka're*)

probably the Italian word meaning 'dear', which has been given as a Christian name in Britain in the 20th century. Another possible source is the Irish meaning 'friend'. There is also a variant **Carita**, derived from the Latin meaning 'beloved'. **Carina** is an Italian diminutive.

CARADOC *m.* (*kerad'ok*)

from the Welsh, meaning 'beloved'. It is common in Wales, but not in other parts of Britain. In the form **Caraticus** it is one of the earliest recorded British names.

CARINA, CARITA *see* CARA

CARL, KARL, CARLA *m. and f.* (*kàl, kà'le*)

the German form of Charles. The name has spread into general use in America, and from there into Britain probably only in the 20th century. The feminine Carla is also thought of as a form of CAROLINE.

CARLO *see* CAROLINE

CARLOTTA *see* CHARLOTTE, LOLA

CARMEL *f.* (ka'm̲e̲l)

from the Hebrew, meaning 'garden', and the name of a famous mountain near the city of Haifa in Israel. St Louis is said to have founded the church and convent on this mountain which, as legend has it, the Virgin Mary and infant Jesus often visited. Variant forms are **Carmela** and **Carmelita**.

CARMEN *f.* (kà'men)

probably the Latin for 'song'. It may also have some connection with the Hebrew for 'garden' (*see* CARMEL). Borrowed from Spain, this name has been used occasionally in Britain since Bizet's opera *Carmen* became popular (first performance 1875). **Charmaine** (*shamān*) is a French equivalent which is also occasionally found.

CAROL f. and m. (kar'el)

from the Irish **Cathal**, and also an anglicized form of the Latin **Carolus** and Slav **Karel**. Its use has spread to Britain from North America. The film director Carol Reed is a famous example, but it is still an uncommon male name. The feminine form was originally a pet form of CAROLINE, but is now a very popular name in its own right.

CAROLINE, CAROLYN f. (karelīn, kar'elin)

from the Italian feminine form of **Carlo**, the equivalent of CHARLES, which was introduced into Britain from Southern Germany by Queen Caroline of Brandenburg-Anspach, wife of George II. It has been very popular since the 18th century. Derivatives are **Carla, Carol, Carola, Carole, Carolina**. Abbreviations include **Carrie, Caddy**, and **Lyn** (*see* CAROL).

CAROLUS *see* CAROL, CHARLES

CARRIE *see* CAROLINE

CARY m. (ka'rē)

a surname which was only rarely used as a first name until it became famous through the film star Cary Grant.

CASEY *m. and f. (kā'sē)*

probably a form of the name **Casimir**, 'proclamation of peace', although it could come from a Celtic word meaning 'valorous'. It is more usual as a boy's than a girl's name.

CASPAR *see* **JASPER**

CASSANDRA *f. (ḳesan'dre)*

In Greek literature this was the name of a prophetic princess of Troy. It first became popular in the Middle Ages with the revival of classical learning and the sympathy which the fate of Troy aroused. The name has continued in use ever since. Also found are **Cassandry** and abbreviations **Cassie** and **Cass**. The latter also occurs as a masculine name.

CATHAL *see* **CAROL**

CATHERINE, CATHARINE *see* **KATHARINE**

CATRIONA *f. (katrē'ōne)*

the Gaelic form of KATHARINE. It was the title of a book by Robert Louis Stevenson, and became very popular in the 19th century as a result of this. **Catrina** is another form of the name.

CECIL, CECILY, CICELY *see* CECILIA

CECIL *m. (ses'il)*

from the Latin, meaning 'blind'. It was the name of a famous Roman clan and was first adopted into English as a girl's name. The popularity of the name in its masculine form only became marked in the 19th century, probably as a result of the influence of the Cecil family. Among the famous members of this family were Lord Burghley, advisor to Queen Elizabeth I, and his son Robert Cecil, whom James I created Earl of Salisbury.

CECILIA *f. (sesē'lie)*

from the Latin meaning 'blind', and the name of the 2nd century martyr and saint, popularly regarded as the patroness of music. The name was first introduced into Britain by the Normans. Variant forms of the name are **Cicely, Cecily, Sisley, Cecil**. The popular shortened form **Celia** probably came into vogue as a result of the character of that name in Shakespeare's play *As You Like It*. Other abbreviated forms are **Sis, Ciss** and **Cissy** or **Sissy** (*see* SHEILA).

CEDRIC *m. (sed'rik)*

from Sir Walter Scott's character in the novel *Ivanhoe*. Scott is said to have mistaken it for Cerdic, who was the founder of the first king of West Saxony. Cedric became popular as a result of the book *Little Lord Fauntleroy* (1886) by F.H. Burnett whose hero bore that name.

CELESTE *f. (selest')*

from the Latin, meaning 'heavenly'. This name and its diminutive **Celestine** are most common in France, where the influence of the 13th century saint, Celestine, may have been greater than in Britain. Celestine has been used in Britain as a masculine name to transliterate the Gaelic Gillaesbuig, also rendered as **Gillespie**.

CELIA *see* CECILIA

CELINA, CELINE *see* SELINA

CENYDD *see* KENNETH

CERDIC *see* CEDRIC

CERI, CERIAN *see* CHERYL

CERIDWEN, KERRIDWEN *f. (kerid'wen)*

from Welsh words for 'poetry' and 'white'. It was the name of a Celtic goddess who was said to inspire poetry. Its use is confined to Wales.

CHAD *m. (chad)*

from the Welsh, meaning 'battle' or 'defence', and the name of a 7th century saint who was Bishop of Lichfield. The name has become popular in America in the 20th century. A famous holder of the name was the Rev. Chad Varah, founder of the Samaritan organisation, which helps those in despair.

CHARIS *f. (kar'is)*

from the Greek, meaning 'grace'. It was first used as a Christian name in the 17th century, although the 16th century poet Edmund Spenser used the name **Charissa** in his *Faerie Queen*. The name has never been popular in Britain.

CHARITY *f. (char'iti)*

from the Latin *caritas,* meaning 'Christian love'. Translated into English as charity, the

name was adopted when it became the custom
for Puritans to name each child after one of
the Christian virtues. The name Charity is
shortened to **Cherry**, and this is still a common
form. Another abbreviation is **Chattie**, used
also for Charlotte.

CHARLENE f. (shà' lēn)

a feminine form of Charles introduced in the
1950s. **Charleen**, **Sharlene** and **Charline** are
also used.

CHARLES m. (chàls)

originally from Old German *carl* or Old English *ceorl*, meaning 'man'. It was latinized as
Carolus and later adapted by the French to
Charles (*shal*). In France the name was very
popular during the Middle Ages due to the
fame of the Emperor Charles the Great or
Charlemagne. The Normans brought the
name to England in the 12th century, but it
did not become popular until its use by the
Royal House of Stuart caused it to be taken
up by Royalists in the 17th century and Jaco-
bites in the 18th century. Its popularity has
continued to increase ever since, especially in
the abbreviated form **Charlie**. **Chas**, originally a written abbreviation, has now come

to be used as a short form. **Chuck** is also used, and in Scotland **Chae** or **Chay** (*see* CAROL, CARL).

CHARLOTTE *f.* (*shà'let*)

the French feminine form of Charles. It was introduced into Britain from France in the early 17th century. George III's wife, Charlotte Sophia of Mecklenburg-Strelitz, popularized the name. Goethe's heroine from the novel *The Sorrows of Werther*, and Princess Charlotte, daughter of George IV, increased the name's popularity. **Carlotta** is the Italian form. Abbreviations are **Lottie, Lotty, Totty** and **Charlie** and **Chattie**.

CHARMAINE *see* CARMEN

CHARMIAN *f.* (*kà'mien, shà'mien*)

from the Greek, meaning 'joy'. Charmian was the name of one of Cleopatra's attendants. Shakespeare's *Antony and Cleopatra* gave the name a wider public, and in the 17th century Dryden used it again in his play on the same subject, *All for Love*. The name has never been widely used.

CHAS *see* CHARLES

CHATTIE *see* **CHARITY, CHARLOTTE**

CHAY *see* **CHARLES**

CHERIE *f. (sherē', she'rē)*

the French word for 'darling'. The forms
Sherry, **Sheree** and **Sherrie** are phonetic
spellings.

CHERRY *see* **CHARITY**

CHERYL *f. (che'rel)*

This may be connected with the Welsh names
Ceri (*m.*) and **Cerian** (*f.*), (*ke'ri, kerie'n*),
meaning 'beloved', but is more probably a form
of the name Cherry (*see* CHARITY). **Cherilyn**
is a development of the name, with **Cher** as a
short form. These names only came into general use in the 1940s, but rapidly became
popular.

CHESTER *m. (ches'te)*

a surname taken from the English town, used
as a first name. The word comes from the Latin
for 'fort'.

CHIP *see* **CHRISTOPHER**

CHLOE f. (klō'i)

from the Greek, meaning 'a green shoot', a name given to the goddess Demeter who protected the green fields. In classical literature it was a pastoral name which was echoed by Elizabethan poets. It was adopted from the New Testament story of the woman of Corinth whom St Paul converted, and is still in use.

CHRIS, CHRISSY see CHRISTABEL, CHRISTINE, CHRISTOPHER

CHRISTABEL f. (kris'tebel)

This Christian name was first used in Britain in the 16th century, and is thought to be a combination of the Latin words *Christus* and *bella,* meaning 'beautiful Christian'. It was the name of a character in Middle English literature, and was used by Thomas Percy in his *Ballad of Sir Cauline.* It was probably from this source that the 19th century poet Coleridge took the name of his heroine, in the poem *Christabel.* It is not a common name in Britain. Abbreviated forms are **Chris, Chrissy** and **Christy**.

CHRISTEN see CHRISTINE

CHRISTIAN *m. and f.* *(kris'tien)*

from the Latin meaning 'Christian'. It has
been used in Britain since the 13th century. It
became more popular after its use by Bunyan
for the hero of *Pilgrim's Progress,* but never
has been as common as the feminine form
CHRISTINE.

CHRISTINE *f.* *(kristēn')*

from the Latin meaning 'a Christian'. **Chris-
tiana** was introduced into Britain in the 13th
century, although the word was not commonly
used as a noun or adjective until the 16th
century. The Old English word, **Christen**, was
in common use before then, but the names
Christina and **Christine** which derive from it
were not popular, though they are now the
commonest forms. The pet name KIRSTY is still
found in Scotland. Abbreviations are **Chrissy**
and **Chris** (*see* TINA).

CHRISTMAS *m. and f.* *(kris'mes)*

taken from the church festival and used to
commemorate the birth of a child on Christmas
Day. The name has been in use since at least
the 13th century, although it has never been
common. A much more popular equivalent is

NOEL. A well-known holder of the name is Mr Christmas Humphreys, the President of the London Buddhist Society.

CHRISTOPHER *m.* (*kris'tefe*)

from the Greek meaning 'bearing Christ', and used originally to describe all Christians. It was first used as a Christian name by the early Christian saint who was believed to have carried the infant Christ to safety across a river. Thus St Christopher became the patron saint of travellers, and the name became common in Roman Catholic countries. The popularity of the name in Britain has fluctuated since the 13th century when it was first used, but it is now fairly common. The Scottish equivalent of the name was **Chrystal** or **Crystal**. Abbreviated forms are **Kester, Kit, Chip, Chris** and **Christie**.

CHRYSEIDA, CRISEYDE *see* **CRESSIDA**

CHRYSTAL *see* **CHRISTOPHER, CRYSTAL**

CHUCK *see* **CHARLES**

CIARAN *see* **KIERAN**

CICELY *see* **CECILIA**

CILLA *see* **PRISCILLA**

CIMMIE *see* **CYNTHIA**

CINDY *f.* (*sindē*)

originally a short form of **Cinderella**, the fairytale heroine who left her drudgery by the hearthside to marry a prince, but now a popular name in its own right. It is also a short form of LUCINDA and CYNTHIA.

CISS, CISSY *see* **CECILIA**

CLAIRE *see* **CLARA**

CLARA, CLARE, CLAIRE *f.* (*kle're, kler*)

from the Latin meaning 'clear' or 'famous'. This name first appeared in the 13th century as Clare. The Italian religious order of the Sisters of St Clara, or 'Poor Clares', founded in the 13th century, was probably responsible for the rapid spread of the name throughout Europe. A variant form is the French **Claire**, popularized by the British film actress Claire

Bloom. Among the many derivatives are **Claribel** and **Clarinda**. An abbreviated form is **Clarrie**.

CLARENCE *m.* (*klar'ens*)

from the dukedom created in the 14th century for King Edward III's son, Lionel, who had married the heiress of Clare in Suffolk (*see* CLARE). It was first used as a Christian name in the early 19th century in Maria Edgeworth's novel *Helen*. It has never been widely used.

CLARIBEL *see* CLARA

CLARICE *f.* (*klar'is*)

from the Latin meaning 'making famous'. The name spread to England from France. The variant form **Clarissa** was made popular in the 18th century by Samuel Richardson's novel *Clarissa Harlowe*. It shares the abbreviation **Clarrie** with Clara.

CLARINDA *see* CLARA

CLARISSA *see* CLARICE

CLARK *m.* (*klak*)

the surname, meaning 'a clerk' used as a first name. Famous users were the actor Clark Gable, and in fiction, Clark Kent, the everyday name for Superman.

CLARRIE *see* CLARA, CLARICE

CLAUD(E) *m.* (*klawd*)

from the name of the Roman clan *Claudius*, derived from the Latin meaning 'lame', or the Greek meaning 'famous'. In homage to the Emperor **Claudius**, under whom Britain was conquered by the Romans, the name was used for both men and women in the 1st and 2nd centuries. Its use soon lapsed in Britain though not in France, and it was from the French that it was taken and revived in Britain in the 16th century by the Scottish family of Hamilton. Lord Claud Hamilton had several French connections. The name is still fairly uncommon. A derivative is **Claudian**, and the pet form **Claudie** is sometimes found.

CLAUDIA *f.* (*klaw'die*)

from the Latin family name *Claudius* and the masculine CLAUD. It has been suggested that the name may have connections with the Welsh GLADYS. Two French diminutives are also used: **Claudette** and **Claudine**, a name made famous by the novels of Colette.

CLAUDIAN, CLAUDIE *see* CLAUD

CLAUDIUS *see* CLAUD

CLAUS *see* NICHOLAS

CLEM, CLEMMIE *see* CLEMENT, CLEMENTINA

CLEMENCE, CLEMENCY *f.* (*klem'ens, klem'ensi*)

from the Latin meaning 'mildness'. The name first appeared in Britain in the 13th century. It is not a common Christian name.

CLEMENT *m.* (*klem'ent*)

from the Latin, meaning 'mild' or 'merciful'. It was the name of an early saint and of several popes. It was popular in Britain from the 12th century until the time of the Reformation, and had a revival in the reign of Queen Victoria. The Christian name was the origin of many surnames, including Clements, Clemens and

Clemson. It has become more popular since the 19th century. Its abbreviated forms are **Clem** and **Clemmie**.

CLEMENTINA, CLEMENTINE *f.*
(klementēne, klementīn)

from the masculine name CLEMENT, with which it shares short forms. It was originally a German adaptation and was most popular during the 19th century. It is rarely used today, except in the well-known song about the Californian Gold Rush in 1849.

CLEO *f.* *(klē'ō)*

from the Greek, meaning 'glory', or 'father's fame'. It is a shortened form of **Cleopatra**. The famous Egyptian queen of this name died in 30 BC. She has been commemorated in many great works of English literature. Probably Shakespeare's play *Antony and Cleopatra* has been most influential in spreading the use of the name.

CLIFFORD *m.* *(klif'ed)*

from the place name, Clifford, of which there are several in Britain. It was used as a surname until the end of the 19th century when it became known as a Christian name. Its abbreviated form is **Cliff**.

CLINTON m. (klin'ten)

a surname meaning 'headland farm', used as a first name. The short form has been given fame by the actor **Clint** Eastwood.

CLIVE m. (klīv)

This name is possibly derived from a village in Shropshire and connected with the word 'cliff'. The name was first used as a Christian name by the 19th century novelist Thackeray for a character in his book *The Newcomes,* and has since been used fairly widely in Britain. Its popularity is largely due to the surname of Robert Clive (Clive of India), especially among families with traditions of service in India.

CLODAGH f. (klōda)

from the name of a river in Ireland. It was first used in the 20th century as a Christian name by the Marquis of Waterford for his daughter. It is in common use only in Ireland.

CLOTILDA f. (klōtil'da)

from a combination of the Old German words for 'loud' and 'battle'. Clotilda was a queen of

France in the 5th and 6th centuries, and she converted her husband, King Clovis (*see* LEWIS), to Christianity. The name is not common.

CLOVIS *see* LEWIS

CLYDE *m.* (klīd)

the Scottish river name, used as a first name.

COELINA *see* SELINA

COINNEACH *see* KENNETH

COLETTE *f.* (kolet')

from the French diminutive of Nicola. It was the name of the reformer of the religious order of 'Poor Clares' in the 15th century, and is popular among Roman Catholics today. The Christian name is the origin of the surnames Colet, Collett, and Colect. The name is best known in this country as the pen-name of a 20th century French writer. It is also spelt **Collette.**

COLIN *m.* (kol'in)

This was originally a French pet form of NICHOLAS. In Scotland it was also interpreted as coming from the Gaelic word *cailean*, meaning 'a young dog' or 'youth'. It is common in Scotland and growing in popularity in England. The Welsh 'collwyn' has the meaning 'hazel grove'. In Switzerland the name Colin Tampon is used as a national nickname.

COLLEEN *f.* (kol'ēn)

from the Irish for 'girl'. The name is not widely used in Britain, but is fairly common in North America.

COLUM, CALUM *m.* (kol'_em_, kal'_em_)

This name was adopted by the Irish from the Latin meaning 'dove'. It was introduced to Scotland in the 6th century with the arrival of St **Columba**, who was also known as **Colum Cillie**, 'Colum of the Church' (*see* MALCOLM). **Calum** and **Colm** are also found.

COMYN *m.* (kom'in)

This name is used occasionally in Scotland and Ireland, but is more common as a surname. It may derive from the Irish for 'crooked', or from the French surname brought to Britain by the Normans.

CONAN m. (kō'nen)

from the Irish, meaning 'high' or 'wisdom'. It was the name of an early Bishop of London. One of the several saints who bore this name is believed to have been an ancestor of the Dukes of Brittany. The name was introduced to England at the time of the Norman Conquest, and was the origin of the surnames Conan, Connant, Connand, Connon and Conning. It was popular from the 12th to 16th centuries but is not very common in Britain today. The most famous holder of the name was Sir Arthur Conan Doyle, creator of Sherlock Holmes.

CONNAIRE see CONNOR

CONNIE see CONSTANCE

CONNOR, CONOR m. (kon'e)

from the Irish, meaning 'strength', 'desire' and possibly 'hound of slaughter'. It was much used in Irish mythology. The Irish form is **Connaire**.

CONRAD m. (kon'rad)

from a compound of the Old German words for 'bold' and 'counsel'. The name is found mostly in Germany where the 13th century Duke Conrad was a greatly beloved figure. His public execution by the conquering Charles of Anjou led to a widespread use of this name in German speaking states. Examples of it have been found in Britain since the 15th century. **Curt** or **Kurt** is a short form used as an independent name.

CONSTANCE, CONSTANTIA *f.* (*kon'stens, konstant'ie*)

from the Latin *constantia*, meaning 'constancy'. The name became popular in many parts of Christendom after Constantine the Great ordered the toleration of Christianity in the Roman Empire, 313 A.D. It was introduced into England at the time of the Norman Conquest, and was adopted by the English as **Custance**. The form **Constancy** was used by the Puritans in the 17th century. Constantia became popular in the 19th century, but today Constance is much more common. Its abbreviation is **Connie**.

CONSTANTINE *m.* (*kon'stantin, kon'stanten*)

from the Latin, meaning 'firm'. It was the name of the first Christian Emperor, and so became popular with Christians. Three Scottish kings were named Constantine after a Cornish saint who was believed to have converted their ancestors to Christianity in the 6th century. It became popular in England from the 12th to the 17th centuries, and was the origin of the surnames Constantine, Considine, Costain and Costin. It is not widely used in Britain today. The composer **Constant** Lambert (1905-51) shows an English form of the name.

CORA *f.* (kaw're)

from the Greek, meaning 'girl'. The name did not appear in Britain until the 19th century, although it was already in use in North America. The diminutive CORINNA has a much longer record of use.

CORAL *f.* (kor'el)

This name reflects the beauty and value of the substance, and has become popular in the 20th century. A French derivative which is also used in Britain is **Coralie**.

CORDELIA *f.* (kawde′lie)

This name first appeared as **Cordeilla** in the 16th century chronicles of Holinshed, from which Shakespeare altered the name to Cordelia for his play *King Lear*. The origin is obscure, but **Cordula** was the Welsh or Cornish name for one of St Ursula's companions. **Kordula** and **Kordel** are the German equivalents.

CORINNA *f. (korin'e̱)*

This name is a diminutive of the Greek word *cora*, meaning 'girl', and a name given to the goddess Persephone, who was associated with the coming of spring. Ovid's use of the name in his love poetry probably inspired its popularity among 17th-century poets, particularly Herrick. **Corinne** is another form of the name, and **Corin** a rare male form.

CORMAC *m. (kaw'me̱k)*

from the Irish, meaning 'a charioteer', a name occurring in Irish legend. Through its prevalence in early Irish history and the Irish Church, the name was accepted as having a Christian character in Ireland. A variant is **Cormick**.

CORNELIA *see* CORNELIUS

CORNELIUS, CORNELIA *m. and f.*
(kawnēl'ies, kawrnē'le)

from the Latin *cornu*, meaning 'horn', and the name of a famous Roman clan. The horn was symbolic of kingship in Roman culture. The name has never been common in Britain. Its abbreviated forms are **Corney, Corny, Cornie** and **Corrie**.

COSMO *m. (koz'mō)*

from the Greek *kosmos*, meaning 'order'. It is the name of one of the patron saints of Milan and was used by the famous Italian family of Medici, in the form **Cosimo**, from the 14th century onwards. It was the name of the 3rd Duke of Gordon who was a friend of **Cosimo** III, Grand Duke of Tuscany, and the name was introduced into several other Scottish families. It is rather uncommon in Britain today.

COURTNEY *m. and f. (kawt'ne)*

an aristocratic surname used as a first name. It comes from **Courtnay**, a French place name.

CRAIG *m. (krag)*

a place and surname meaning 'crag', which has become very popular since the 1940s.

CRESSIDA *f.* (*kres'ide*)

Taken from Greek literature, the name **Briseida** was used by the 12th century French playwright Benoit for his faithless Trojan heroine. It was adapted by the 15th century Italian writer Boccaccio to **Chryseida**, in his retelling of the story. Chaucer used the name **Criseyde**, and Shakespeare changed it to Cressida or **Cressid**. Despite the fictional character's bad reputation, the name has recently become popular. An abbreviated form is **Cressy**.

CRISPIN, CRISPIAN, *m.* (*kris'pen, kris'pien*)

from the Latin *crispus*, meaning 'curled'. The 3rd century martyrs **Crispinus** and **Crispinianus** were the patron saints of shoemakers. The name was popular in Britain in the Middle Ages and has recently enjoyed a revival.

CRYSTAL *f.* (*kris'tl*)

another jewel name, this is simply the word used as a first name. It is also spelt **Chrystal** and the form **Krystal** has become known through the television series *Dynasty*. As a man's name it is a pet form of CHRISTOPHER.

CUDBERT *see* **CUTHBERT**

CUDDY *see* **CUTHBERT**

CURT *see* **CONRAD**

CURTIS m. (*ke'tis*)

a surname, from the French meaning 'courteous', used as a first name.

CUSTANCE *see* **CONSTANCE**

CUTHBERT m. (*kuth'bet*)

from the Old English words *cuth* and *beorht*, meaning 'famous' and 'bright'. It was in common use both before and after the Norman Conquest, and was the name of the 7th century saint and Bishop of Lindisfarne in Northumbria. It sometimes appeared as **Cudbert**, and had the pet form **Cuddy**. The name fell out of use from just after the Reformation until the 19th century, when it was brought back by the Oxford Movement. It was a slang term for someone who avoided military service during the 1914-18 War, and it may be partly due to this usage that the name is not popular today. The school 'swot' in the *Beano*'s Bash Street Kids is called Cuthbert Cringeworthy.

CY *see* CYRIL, CYRUS

CYBILL *see* SIBYL

CYNTHIA *f.* (*sin'thie*)

from one of the titles of the Greek Goddess Artemis, meaning 'of Mount Cynthus'. The name first became known through its use by the Latin poet Propertius, and it was very popular among Elizabethan poets. Mrs Gaskell's character in her novel *Wives and Daughters* brought it back into favour during the late 19th century, since when it has become fairly common. Pet forms include **Cindy** and the rare **Cimmie**.

CYPRIAN *m.* (*sip'rien*)

from the Latin Cyprianus, meaning 'from Cyprus'. It was the name of a famous Latin writer, who was a Christian martyr in the 3rd century. The form **Cyprianus** has also been used occasionally in Britain.

CYRIL m. (sir'el)

probably from the Greek *kyrios*, meaning
'lord'. There were two saints of this name in
the 4th and 5th centuries, and it was a 9th
century saint Cyril who took Christianity to
the Slavs, and devised the Cyrillic alphabet.
The name was first used in England in the
17th century, but did not become common until
the 19th century. The name shares its only
abbreviation **Cy** with Cyrus. There is a rare
feminine form **Cyrilla**.

CYRUS m. (sī'res)

from a Greek form of the Persian word meaning 'sun' or 'throne'. This is the name of the
founder of the Persian Empire in the 6th century BC. It was first used in Britain in the 17th
century among Puritans, probably in honour of
the fact that the Emperor Cyrus allowed the
Jews to return to Palestine from the Baby-
lonian captivity. It is now popular in North
America, where common diminutive forms are
Cy and **Cyro**.

D

DAFYDD *see* **DAVID**

DAGMAR *m. and f.* (*dag'mà*)

a Danish name possibly meaning 'joy of the Dane'. It has spread into North America through Danish immigrant families. It is more common as a female name.

DAI *see* **DAVID**

DAISY *f.* (*dā'zi*)

a 19th-century pet name for MARGARET, using the English name for the same flower as the French Marguerite. It is sometimes used independently, but is not popular today.

DALE *m. and f.* (*dāl*)

from the Old English for 'valley'. At first more common as a girl's name, it is now more frequently used for boys. Dale Carnegie, the

American writer, may have helped to make it better known as a masculine name.

DAMARIS f. (dam'ēris)

from the Greek name in the New Testament of an Athenian woman converted by St Paul. Adopted by Puritans in the 17th century, it is rare today.

DAMHNAIT see DYMPHNA

DAMIAN, DAMIEN m. (dā'mien)

from the Greek, meaning 'tamer'. There have been four saints called by this name. It was little used before this century, but has been very popular since the 1970s.

DAMON m. (dā'men)

from the Greek, meaning 'rule' or 'guide'. According to Greek legend, Damon and Pythias were inseparable friends, who were ready to die for each other. It is perhaps best known through the American writers Damon Runyan and Damon Knight.

DAN, DANNY see DANIEL

DANA m. and f. (dà'ne)

The masculine form of this name comes from
the Old English word for a Dane, and is sometimes found in the form **Dane**. The actor Dana
Andrews made it well known, but it is now
unusual as a man's name. The feminine name,
now widely used, is a Scandinavian form of the
name DANIEL, although some uses of it may
come from the Irish fertility goddess, Danu.

DANDY see ANDREW

DANIEL m., DANIELLE f. (dan'iel, daniel')

the Hebrew name of the Old Testament
prophet, meaning 'God has judged'. It is found
in England before the Norman Conquest, but
only among priests and monks. It became
more widespread in the 13th and 14th
centuries. In Ireland and Wales it is often
found as a transliteration of the Irish
Domhnall (see DONALD) and Welsh **Deiniol**,
meaning 'attractive' or 'charming'. Its
shortened forms are **Dan** and **Danny**. The
feminine **Danielle** comes from the French,
while **Daniella**, another form of the name,
seems to be a coinage of the 1960s.

DANTE m. (dan'te)

an Italian name, famous through the 13th-century poet Dante Alighieri. Its use as a given name is rare and is probably entirely due to the reputation of this poet and of the poet Dante Gabriel Rossetti (1828-82). The name is an abbreviation of **Durante** or **Durand** (du'rend), meaning 'enduring'.

DAPHNE f. (daf'ni)

from the Greek for a 'bay' or 'laurel bush'. In classical mythology it was the name of a nymph whom the god Apollo loved. In seeking to escape him she called on the gods for help, and was changed by them into a bush. The name was used mainly for dogs until the turn of the century, when it became quite common as a Christian name. A famous modern example is the novelist Daphne Du Maurier.

DARBY, DERBY m. (dà'bi)

The etymology of this name is uncertain. It appears mainly in Ireland and is possibly a shortened form of the Irish Diarmid (see DERMOT), meaning 'free man'. It may also derive from the Norse meaning 'deer park'. Darby and Joan, the proverbial name for a loving old couple, probably originated in an 18th-century ballad.

D'ARCY *m.* (*dà'si*)

The English family of this name was founded by Norman d'Arcei, one of William the Conqueror's companions. A branch of the family went to Ireland, where Darcy was adopted as a Christian name, possible to transliterate the Irish **Dorchaidh** ('dark man'). A variant form is **Darsey**.

DARREL(L), DAR(R)YL *m. and f.* (*dar'el*)

from the Old English word meaning 'darling'. Darryl F. Zanuck, the film producer, may have helped to make the name better known. It is only rarely found as a feminine name.

DARREN *m.* (*da'ren*)

from a surname of unknown meaning. This name seems to have been introduced in the 1950s and has been very popular since the 1960s.

DARSEY *see* D'ARCY

DATHI *see* DAVID

DAVID m. (dā'vid)

the Hebrew name of the second king of Israel
in the Old Testament, meaning 'beloved'. This
name absorbed the Celtic form **Dathi**
('nimble') and became very popular in Wales
and Scotland. The Welsh patron saint is a 6th-
century David. There were two Scottish kings
of this name in the 10th and 14th centuries.
The name did not appear in England before
the Norman Conquest, but it was a common
medieval surname in the variant forms **Davy**,
Davit and **Deakin**. It has been a common
name for centuries and its popularity shows
no sign of decreasing. Short forms are **Dave**,
Davy, **Davie** and in Wales **Dafydd** becomes
Dai or **Taffy**, the latter being the common
British nickname for a Welshman.

DAVIDA, DAVINA f. (davē'de, davē'ne)

Scottish feminine forms of DAVID, these are
found from the 17th century, but are not
common. **Davita** and **Davinia** are also found.

DAWN f. (dawn)

This name came into being in the late 19th
century. The Latin AURORA had been in vogue
slightly earlier, and the English form was

probably entirely a literary invention. It has been popular among film stars, and has therefore gained publicity and a large following in recent years.

DEAN m. (dēn)

a surname, meaning 'valley', adopted as a first name. It seems to have become popular in the United States first, but has been widely used here since the 1960s. Dean Martin (b. Dino Corcetti) is a well-known user of the name.

DEANNE, DEANNA see DIANA

DEBBIE see DEBORAH

DEBORAH f. (deb'awre)

from the Hebrew meaning 'bee', and the name of a prophetess and poet in the Old Testament. It was first used by Puritans in the 17th century. **Debbie** or **Debby** is a common abbreviation which is sometimes used independently. **Debra** is a modern spelling of the name.

DECIMUS m. DECIMA f. (des'imes, des'ime)

from the Latin *decimus*, meaning 'tenth', this was used in Victorian times as a name for the tenth child in large families. Decima was used for girls and is sometimes still used in smaller families. Decimus Burton (1800-81) was a noted architect.

DECLAN m. (dek'len)

the name of an Irish saint associated with Ardmore. It has recently been popular with Irish parents.

DEE m. and f. (de)

This is usually a nickname, given to anyone with a name beginning with the letter D, but is occasionally found as a given name. Compounds such as **Deedee** also occur.

DEINIOL see DANIEL

DEIRDRE f. (dēr'dri)

the Irish name of a character in Irish and Scottish legend, possibly meaning 'raging' or 'sorrowful'. Beautiful and wise 'Deirdre of the sorrows', as she is sometimes called, left Ireland in order to marry the man of her choice, and lived with him and his two brothers near Loch Etive. Tempted back to Ireland by a false offer of friendship, the three men were killed, and Deirdre, lamenting her sad lot, committed suicide. The name became popular after the late 19th-century Celtic revival.

DELIA f. (dē'lie̱)

This name is derived from Delos, the legendary birthplace of the Greek moon goddess Artemis (see ARTEMISIA). It was popular with pastoral poets in the 17th and 18th centuries and is still used occasionally.

DELLA f. (dèl'e̱)

Originally a short form of ADELA, this is now well established as a name in its own right.

DEMELZA f. (de̱mel'za)

a place name, meaning 'the hill-fort of Maeldaf', used as a first name in Cornwall. It has become more widely known through its use in the *Poldark* books and television series.

DENHOLM m. (den'ulm)

a place-name, meaning 'island valley', used as a first name. The actor Denholm Elliot is a well-known example. The similar **Denham**, 'home in a valley', is also used.

DENIS, DENNIS *m.*, DENISE *f.* (*den'is, denèz'*)

a derivation of Dionysos, who was the Greek god of wine and revelry. Denis is the French form and the name of the patron saint of France. It occurs in England from the 12th century on and is very popular today. In Ireland it has long been used as a substitute for the Irish Donnchadh (*see* DUNCAN). **Den** and **Denny** are short forms. **Denise**, the feminine form, is also from French. **Dion** (*m.*) and **Dionne** (*f.*) also come from Dionysos and are growing in popularity.

DENZIL *m.* (*den'zil*)

Spelt Denzell, this is an old Cornish family name derived from a place-name. In the 17th century it came by marriage into the Holles family who adopted it as a Christian name. It is still used by the Holles family and in Cornwall. Denzil Davies, the politician, is a holder of the name.

DERBY *see* DARBY

DEREK, DERRICK *m.* (*der'ik*)

a derivation of Old German THEODORIC, or 'people's ruler'. It occurs in the 15th century but has only become popular in the last century. Its fall from favour between these two periods is attributed to the notorious 17th-century hangman of that name. Variant forms recently revived are **Deryk**, **Deric** and the Dutch form **Dirk**, popularized by the well-known film star Dirk Bogarde. Pet forms are **Derry** and **Rick** or **Rickie**.

DERIC, DERYK *see* DEREK

DERMOT *m.* (*der'mot*)

This is the anglicized spelling of **Diarmit**, **Diarm(a)id**, the Irish name meaning 'free from envy', or 'free man'. The legendary character who bore this name eloped with a queen of Tara. He was caught by the husband and forced to hunt a wild boar, thus meeting his death. A shortened form is DARBY.

DERRY *see* DEREK

DERVLA *f.* (*der'vle*)

This is an old Irish name meaning 'true desire'. It is best known from the travel writer Dervla Murphy.

DÉSIRÉE f. (dāzē'rā)

a French name meaning 'desired'. It has been borrowed from the French, with the pronunciation retained.

DESMOND m. (dez'mend)

from Irish Deas-Mumhain, meaning 'man of South Munster'. It was originally used as a surname in Ireland. Later it became a Christian name, and came to England in the late 19th century. **Des** and **Desi** are short forms.

DIAM(A)ID see DERMOT

DIANA f. (dīan'e)

the Latin name of the Roman Goddess equivalent to the Greek Artemis (see ARTEMISIA). She was the feminine counterpart of Janus, the sun god, and associated with the moon and virginity. She was also the goddess of hunting and protector of wild animals. Its use as a Christian name dates from the Renaissance, when the French form **Diane** is also first found. Both names are still popular. **Di** is the commonest short form, as seen in the popular nickname for the Princess of Wales. The actress

Deanna Durbin introduced a different form of the name, and the form **Deanne** is also found. DINAH is a separate name.

DIARMAID, DIARMID, DIARMIT *see* DARBY, DERMOT

DICK, DICKE, DICKIE, DICKON *see* RICHARD

DIGBY *m. (dig′bi)*

a place and surname, meaning 'the settlement by the dike', used as a first name.

DILYS *f. (dil′is)*

from the Welsh meaning 'perfect', 'genuine'. The name became current in Wales in the 19th century, and is now used throughout Britain. **Dilly** is a short form.

DINAH *f. (dī′ne)*

from the Hebrew, meaning 'lawsuit' or 'judged'. It was the name of one of Jacob's daughters in the Old Testament. It came into use in the 17th century among the Puritans and was a favourite name in the 19th century, when it was often confused with DIANA. Nowadays it is also spelt **Dina**.

DION, DIONNE, DIONYSOS *see* **DENIS**

DIRK *see* **DEREK**

DODIE, DODO *see* **DOROTHEA**

DOLAN *m.* (*dōlen*)
___
from the Irish meaning 'black-haired'.

DOLL, DOLLY *see* **DOROTHEA**

DOLORES *f.* (*dolaw'rez*)
___
This name was originally a short form of the Spanish, Maria de Dolores, or 'Mary of the Sorrows', after the feast of the 'Seven Sorrows of Our Lady'. It is one of several 'festival' names common in Roman Catholic countries. **Mercedes** (Our Lady of the Mercies) and NOEL are two others occasionally used in Britain. The name became popular in North America about 1930. Pet forms are LOLA, **Lolita** and **Lo**.

DOMHNALL, DOMNALL *see* **DANIEL, DOMINIC, DONALD**

DOMINIC(K) *m.*, **DOMINIQUE** *f. (dom'inik, dominēk')*

from the Latin *dominicus*, meaning 'of the Lord'. It is possible that the name was first used for children born on the Sabbath day. It was used in England as a monk's name before the Norman Conquest and probably became more widespread on account of St Dominic, founder of the Order of Preachers known as the Black Friars (early 13th century). Until this century it was used almost exclusively by Roman Catholics, but is now widely used. In Ireland it is occasionally used as a substitute for the Irish Domhnall (*see* DONALD). Dominique, from the French, is now the most popular feminine form, although **Dominica** is a rare feminine form.

DONALD *m. (don'eld)*

from the Irish Domnall, meaning 'world mighty', through the Gaelic form Domhnall (*daw'nal*). The name is very common in the Scottish Highlands, and **Donal** is much used in Ireland, where it is interchangeable with DANIEL. The name was borne by six Scottish kings. Common short forms are **Don** and **Donny**.

DONNA *f.* (*don'e*)

This is the Italian word for 'lady'. It has been used as a Christian name in the 20th century, particularly in North America.

DONNCHADH *see* **DENIS**

DONOVAN *m.* (*don'even*)

a Celtic surname, meaning 'dark brown', used as a first name. It gained publicity as the name of a popular singer who had a number of hits in the 1960s.

DORA *f.* (*daw're*)

Originally this name was a diminutive of DOROTHY and also of THEODORA, but it is now a name in its own right. It came into use at the beginning of the 19th century. A pet form is **Dorrie**, shared with other names like DOREEN and DORIS.

DORAN *m.* (*daw'ren*)

an Irish name, meaning 'stranger, exile', which has recently become more popular.

DORCAS f. (daw'kes)

from the Greek, meaning 'gazelle'. In the New
Testament it was used as a Greek translation
for the Aramaic TABITHA, the name of the
woman raised from the dead by St Peter. The
name was later used to describe groups of
women who made clothes for the needy. Both
names were popular in the 17th century
among the Puritans, but are now very rare.

DORCHAIDH see D'ARCY

DOREEN f. (daw'rēn, dawrēn')

from the Irish Doirean, possibly an adaptation
of DOROTHY. Some sources derive it from the
Celtic word for 'sullen'. It came into general
use in Britain at the beginning of the 20th
century with the Celtic revival and the appear-
ance of the name in literature inspired by the
Irish revolutionary movement. A short form is
Dorrie.

DORIAN m. (do'rien)

from the ancient Greek people known as the
Dorians who originated in the northern Greek
area called Doris but later dominated the
south of the country. The best-known group

were the Spartans. The word was introduced as a first name by Oscar Wilde in his *The Picture of Dorian Gray* (1891). The sports commentator Dorian Williams is a modern example of the name.

DORINDA *f.* (*dawrin'de*)

This name was invented in the 18th century as a poetic variation of DORA and DOROTHY. Many other forms, like BELINDA and Clarinda, (*see* CLARA) were invented at this time.

DORIS *f.* (*dor'is*)

This is the name of a sea nymph in Greek mythology. Its meaning is unknown, though it probably has connections with the Dorian people of Greece. In classical literature it was a poetic name. It came into use at the end of the 19th century and is still fairly common.

DOROTHEA, DOROTHY *f.* (*dorothē'e, do'rothi*)

from the Greek meaning 'gift of God'. The name is found in Britain from the end of the 15th century and has been in use ever since. In the 16th century it was abbreviated to **Doll(y)**, and was so popular that the common plaything of young girls was called after it. In Scotland a doll is sometimes called a **Dorrity**. Shakespeare's character Doll Tearsheet, and its use in this form as a name for an immoral woman, caused it to fall into disfavour for a time. Later short forms are DORA, **Dot**, **Dottie**, **Dodo**, **Dodie** and **Thea**. An unusual shortened form was used by Charles Dickens for his novel *Little Dorrit* (*see also* THEODORA).

DORRIE *see* DORA, DOREEN, DORIS

DORRIT, DORRITY *see* DOROTHEA

DOT, DOTTIE *see* DOROTHEA

DOUG, DOUGIE *see* DOUGLAS

DOUGAL, DUGAL(D) *m.* (dŏo'gal)

from the Irish *dubh gall*, meaning 'black stranger', a name given by the Irish to the Norwegians and still used to describe an Englishman. It is quite a common first name in the Scottish Highlands, and is often used as a lowland nickname for a Highlander.

DOUGLAS *m.* (*dug'les*)

from the Gaelic *dubh glas*, meaning 'dark blue' or grey. It was first a Celtic river name, then the surname of a powerful Scottish family, famous for their strength and bravery in fighting, and from about the late 16th century a first name for both girls and boys. It is still a common name for boys, especially in Scotland. **Duggie**, **Dougie** and **Doug** are pet forms.

DOWSABEL *see* DULCIE

DREW *m.* (*dróo*)

from the Old French, meaning 'sturdy', possibly through the Old German for 'strength' or Old German **Drogo** meaning 'to carry' or 'to bear'. The name was brought to Britain by the Normans and also occurs in Old Welsh. It is a fairly unusual name but is sometimes used as an abbreviation for ANDREW.

DRUSILLA *f.* (*dróo'sil'e*)

a feminine diminutive of the Latin Drusus, a Roman clan name. It occurs in the New Testament and was adopted in the 17th century by Puritans. It is still used occasionally, mainly in North America.

DRYSTAN *see* **TRISTRAM**

DUANE, DWAYNE *m. (dwān)*

an Irish surname, probably meaning 'black', used as a first name. The pop singer Duane Eddy made the name better known in the 1950s.

DUDLEY *m. (dud'li)*

originally a surname derived from the place of that name in Worcestershire. The Dudley family rose to power under the Tudors. Robert Dudley, Earl of Leicester, was the favourite of Queen Elizabeth for many years. Like other aristocratic names it was adopted for general use as a first name in the 19th century. **Dud** is used as a short form.

DUGAL(D) *see* **DOUGAL**

DUGGIE *see* **DOUGLAS**

DUKE *see* **MARMADUKE**

DULCIEBELLA *see* **DULCIE**

DULCIE f. (dul'si)

This name is a recent derivation from the Latin *dulcis,* meaning 'sweet', and is not from the Latin name **Dulcibella**, which is the source of **Dowsabel**, the 14th-17th century variant. Dulcibella was used in the 18th century and Dulcie appears in the late 19th century.

DUNCAN m. (dun'ken)

from the Irish **Donnchadh**, meaning 'brown warrior'. It was the name of two Scottish kings and at one time was almost entirely confined to Scotland. The Irish equivalent is DENIS.

DUNSTAN m. (dun'sten)

from the Old English compound *dun*, meaning 'hill', and *stan*, meaning 'stone'. It was the name of a famous 10th-century Archbishop of Canterbury. It appears from time to time before the Reformation, and was revived by the Oxford Movement in the 19th century.

DURAND, DURANTE *see* DANTE

DUSTIN m. (dustin)

Best known from the actor Dustin Hoffman, this name is currently very popular in the

United States. It may be from a place name, meaning 'dusty', or could be a form of THURSTAN.

DWAYNE see DUANE

DWIGHT m. (dwīt)

originally an English surname. The use of this name as a Christian name in the United States probably arose through Timothy Dwight, President of Yale University 1795-1817. The 20th-century U.S. President, Dwight D. Eisenhower gave a wider circulation to the name.

DYLAN m. (dilen)

This is the name of a legendary Welsh hero, son of the sea god, possibly meaning 'son of the wave'. It was rare outside Wales, but the Welsh poet Dylan Thomas made the name more familiar to the general public. The singer Bob Dylan, often referred to by his second name alone, took his stage name from the poet and may have helped its popularity.

DYMP(H)NA f. (dimf'ne, dimp'ne)

the anglicized form of the Irish **Damhnait**, the name of an Irish virgin martyr. It possibly means 'one fit to be'.

E

EACHAN *see* **HECTOR**

EADGYTH *see* **EDITH**

EALDFRITH *see* **ALFRED**

EAMON(N) *see* **EDMOND**

EARL *m.* (*erl*)

from the Old English, meaning a 'nobleman' or 'chief'. This British title has been used as a first name in the last hundred years, mainly in North America. Erle is a variant spelling, as in the author Erle Stanley Gardner.

EARNEST *see* **ERNEST**

EARTHA *f.* (*er'the*)

from Old English *eorthe*, meaning 'earth'. A well-known modern example is Eartha Kitt, the singer and actress, but the name is rather uncommon.

EBENEZER m. (ebenē′ze)

from the Hebrew, meaning 'stone of help'. In the Old Testament it is the name of a stone which Samuel placed between Mizpah and Shen and called Ebenezer, in memory of the triumph of the Jews over the Philistine army. It was first used as a Christian name in the 17th century among Puritans. It is now used mainly in North America, with the shortened form **Eben**.

ECTOR see **HECTOR**

ED, EDDIE see **EDGAR, EDMOND EDWARD**

EDA see **ADA**

EDAN, EDANA see **EDNA**

EDEN m. and f. (ē′den)

from the Hebrew, meaning 'delight'. Like other Old Testament place names it has been used as a Christian name since the 17th century, when the Puritans first adopted it, but has never been common.

EDGAR *m.* (ed'ge)

from the Old English meaning 'happy spear'.
Owing to the popularity of King Edgar, King
Alfred's grandson, the name continued in use
after the Norman Conquest, but it faded out
at the end of the 13th century. It was used by
Shakespeare for a character in *King Lear*, and
revived with other Old English names by 18th-
century writers of fiction. Its great popularity
in the 19th century probably stems from its
use for the hero of Scott's novel *The Bride
of Lammermoor*. It is a fairly unusual name,
sometimes shortened to **Ed** or **Eddie**.

EDIE *see* EDITH

EDINA *see* EDNA

EDITH *f.* (ē'dith)

from the Old English name Eadgyth, meaning
'prosperous war'. There were at least two English saints of that name in the 10th century.
The name survived the Norman Conquest and
was probably adopted by the Normans and
used to transliterate several English names.
Edith was in use throughout the Middle Ages,
after which it became rather rare, but it returned to favour in the 19th century. Among

the many famous 20th-century holders of the name are the heroic nurse Edith Cavell, Dame Edith Sitwell the poet and Dame Edith Evans the actress. The name is often shortened to **Edie**.

EDMOND, EDMUND *m. (ed'mend)*

from the Old English Eadmund, meaning 'happy protection'. It was the name of two kings of England and of two saints. Edmond is the French form which was used from the late Middle Ages, **Eamon(n)** is the Irish form. It has remained in use till the present day but is now less popular than it was in the 19th century. It has been made famous by Sir Edmund Hilary, the New Zealand mountaineer who conquered Everest. Shortened forms are **Ed**, **Eddie** and **Ted**.

EDNA *f. (ed'ne)*

The etymology of this name is obscure. It may be derived from the obsolete Old English name **Edana**, meaning 'happiness' or 'rich gift'. Another possibility exists in a feminine form of the Celtic name **Edan** meaning 'fire'. It may also derive from another obsolete Old English name **Edina**, which is probably a feminine form of EDWIN. The name occurs several times in the Apocrypha and its Hebrew meaning is probably 'rejuvenation'. The modern use of it may stem from the popularity of the novelist Edna Lyall in the late 19th century.

EDWARD m. (ed'wed)

from the Old English, meaning 'rich guardian'. Edward the Confessor established its popularity in England and ensured its survival after the Norman Conquest. It was further strengthened by the accession of Edward I, after which there was an Edward on the English throne for over a hundred years. It has remained popular in Britain ever since. The youngest of Queen Elizabeth II's four children is called Edward and this undoubtedly made the name more popular in the 1960s. The short forms **Ned** and **Ted** have been used since the 14th century, but **Ed** or **Eddie** is more common today, together with **Neddy** and **Teddy**.

EDWIN m., EDWINA f. (ed'win, edwē'ne)

from the Old English, meaning 'rich friend'. It is the name of the first Christian king of Northumbria in the 7th century, who is said to have given it to the city of Edinburgh. The name survived the Norman Conquest and became popular in the 18th century. It was quite common in the 19th century, and Dickens used the name for the title of his last novel, *Edwin Drood*. It is still used occasionally. Edwina is a modern feminine form recently given much publicity by the politician Edwina Currie.

EFFIE *see* EUPHEMIA

EGBERT *m.* (*eg' bet*)

from the Old English, meaning 'sword bright', the name of the first King of all England and of a 7th-century Northumbrian saint who was very influential in Ireland. It enjoyed some degree of popularity in the 19th century, but is now rarely found.

EIBHILIN *see* EVELINE

ELEANORE, ELEANORA *see* ELINOR

EILEEN, AILEEN *f.* (*ī' lēn*)

probably a development of EVELYN. In Ireland it is often used as the equivalent of HELEN. Like other Irish names it spread throughout Britain at the beginning of the 20th century. **Eily** and **Eilidh** are short forms.

EITHNE see **AITHNE**

ELAINE f. (ēlān')

an Old French form of HELEN, which occurs in medieval literature. It came into general use through the popularity of Tennyson's *Idylls of the King* (1859), which is based on Malory's *Morte D'Arthur* and which includes the story of *Lancelot and Elaine*. There is also a Welsh name **Elain**, meaning 'fawn'.

ELEANOR(A) see **ELINOR**

ELENA, ELLEN see **HELEN**

ELI m. (ē'lī)

from the Hebrew, meaning 'height', and the name of the high priest in the Old Testament who looked after the prophet Samuel in the Temple. It was adopted as a first name in the 17th century. It is also a shortened form of ELIAS, Eliza and Elihu ('God is the Lord').

ELIAS, ELIJAH m. (ēlī'es, ēlī'je)

from the Hebrew, meaning 'Jehovah is God'. Both forms were very common in the Middle Ages, with the diminutives **Ellis** and **Eliot** which became surnames. Elijah regained popularity with the Puritans in the 17th century, but neither form is much used today. However, El(l)iot has recently become quite common as a first name.

ELIHU *see* **ELI**

ELINOR, ELEANORE, ELEANOR(A) *f.*
(*el'ene, elenor'e*)

These are forms of HELEN, derived from French and introduced by Eleanor of Aquitaine, who married Henry II. It was popular in the Middle Ages, and was further strengthened when Edward I erected beautiful stone crosses in memory of his wife, Eleanor of Castile, who died in 1290. It has been used ever since, often in its shortened form **Nell**. A famous modern holder of the name was Eleanor Roosevelt, philanthropist wife of the former U.S. President (*see* NORA).

EL(L)IOT *see* **ELIAS**

ELISABET, ELIZABETHA, ELISE *see* **ELIZABETH**

ELISHA m. (eli′she)

from the Hebrew, meaning 'God is salvation'. This Biblical name was used mostly by Puritans in the 17th century in Britain, and is still current in North America.

ELISHEBA see **ELIZABETH**

ELIZA see **ELI, ELIZABETH**

ELIZABETH, ELISABETH f. (ēliz′ebeth)

from the Hebrew **Elisheba**, meaning 'oath of God' or 'God has sworn'. The present form developed from the Greek **Elisabet** through the Latin **Elizabetha** to Elizabeth. In Britain the 'z' form is usual, on the Continent the 's' is used. It was first used as a Christian name in the Eastern Church, and found its way across Europe to France, where it had the form ISABEL. This was also the usual medieval form in England. Elizabeth became common about the end of the 15th century, and its later popularity in England stemmed from the long reign of Elizabeth I. Among the many diminutives the following have been most used: **Bess(ie)**, **Betsy, Betty, Beth, Eliza, Lizzy, Liz, Libby** and the Scottish **Elspeth, Elspie** and **Elsie**, which are now used independently. The

German ELSA, LISA, **Liesel**, the Italian BETTINA, and the French **Elise**, **Lisette** and **Babette**, are also used in Britain.

ELKE *f.* (el'_ke_)

a German pet form of the name ALICE, made known by the actress Elke Sommer and, in a slightly different form, by the singer **Elkie Brooks**.

ELLA *f.* (el'_e_)

a name used by the Normans, but probably derived from the Old German Alia, meaning 'all'. It may also be a variant of ELLEN or ELINOR. It was revived in the 19th century and is now fairly common. A well-known example is the jazz singer Ella Fitzgerald.

ELLEN *f.* (el'_en_)

This is an older English form of HELEN, now used independently. It is especially popular in Scotland and Ireland.

ELLIS *see* **ELIAS**

ELMER *m.* (el'_me_)

This name is derived either from **Aylmer** or the Old English **Ethelmer**, and means 'noble'.

Its use in the U.S. may stem from two brothers with the surname Elmer, who were prominent in the American War of Independence.

ELSA, ELSIE *f. (el'se, el'si)*

The probable source of Elsa is the Old German meaning 'noble one'. However, both names are used as abbreviations of ELIZABETH, and Elsie is sometimes the short form of ALISON. Elsie was originally Scottish and is the more common form in Britain. Elsa is the heroine of Richard Wagner's opera *Lohengrin* and this made the name popular in the 19th century.

ELSPETH, ELSPIE *see* ELIZABETH

ELTON *m. (el'ten)*

a surname, probably meaning 'Ella's settlement', used as a first name. The singer Elton John is a well-known example.

ELUNED *f. (eli'ned)*

This is a Welsh name connected with the word for 'idol'. It is seldom used outside Wales. The short form **Luned** is the origin of LYNETTE.

ELVIRA *f. (elvēr'e)*

a Spanish name, possibly derived from an Old German word meaning 'elf counsel'. It has been used occasionally since the beginning of the 19th century. It is perhaps best known as the name of the ghost in Noel Coward's play *Blithe Spirit* and from the Swedish film *Elvira Madigan*.

ELVIS *m. (el'vis)*

a name that was almost unknown until given world fame by Elvis Presley. It is probably a version of the name of the Irish saint Ailbhe (*elve*), found in Wales in the form St Elvis, rather than from the Scandinavian 'all-wise', as has also been suggested.

EMANUEL *m. (ēman'ūel)*

from the Hebrew meaning 'God with us'. It was the name given to the promised Messiah by the prophet Isaiah in the Old Testament. It was first used as a first name by the Greeks in the form **Manuel**. This is also the Spanish form. Both Emanuel and Manuel were found in Cornwall in the 15th and 16th centuries. The veteran politician **Manny** Shinwell shows the short form of the name.

EMBLEN, EMBLIN *see* EMMELINE

EMERALD *see* ESMERALDA(H)

EMILY, EMILIA *f. (em'ili, emēlie)*

from the Latin Aemelius (*see* AMELIA), the
name of a Roman plebeian clan. Boccaccio,
the 14th-century Italian writer, used **Emilia**,
popularizing this form in the Middle Ages, and
Chaucer borrowed it in the form **Emelye**. The
name has persisted since then, becoming very
common as Emily in the 19th century, when
it was sometimes shortened to EMMA. **Milly** is
another short form. It is sometimes used as a
form of Amelia.

EMLYN *m. and f. (em'lin)*

a common Welsh name, possibly derived from
the Latin Aemilianus. It is also found as an
English feminine name derived from the Old
German meaning 'serpent of work'.

EMMA *f. (em'e)*

from a shortened form of an Old German compound of *ermin*, meaning 'universal', as in the
name **Ermyntrude**, 'universal strength'. It
was introduced into England by Emma,

125

daughter of Richard I, Duke of Normandy. The 11th-century Queen Emma was a very popular figure called 'the fair maid of Normandy'. The English form was **Em(m)**, and this was used until the mid-18th century, when the original form was revived. Jane Austen's novel *Emma* (1816) has also been influential. Today Emma is one of the commonest girl's names. **Emmy** is a pet form.

EMMELINE *f.* (*em'elēn*)

from the Old French diminutives of Emilia and EMILY. The Normans introduced the name to England in the 11th century in many variant forms, like **Emblem** and **Emblin**, but Emmeline is the one most often found. The suffragette leader, Mrs Pankhurst (1858-1928) was an Emmeline.

EMRYS *see* AMBROSE

ENA *f.* (*ē'ne*)

an anglicized form of the Irish AITHNE. Its popularity in England is probably partly due to Princess Ena, who was born in 1887, and who became Queen of Spain. It is also possibly derived from the Greek word meaning 'praise', as the feminine form of AENEAS.

ENID f. (ē'nid, en'id)

This is a Welsh name, meaning 'life, soul', that
came into use in England in the 19th century,
through Tennyson's poem *Geraint and Enid* in
the *Idylls of the King* (1859).

ENOCH m. (ē'nok)

from the Hebrew, meaning 'trained', 'skilled'
or 'dedicated'. It was the name of an Old Testament patriarch and was adopted in the 17th
century by the Puritans. Tennyson's *Enoch
Arden* (1864) may have helped to preserve
it, but it is now rare. A well-known modern
example is Enoch Powell, the politician.

EOGHAN see **EVAN**

EPHRAIM m. (ē'frām, ē'frem)

from the Hebrew, meaning 'fruitful', an Old
Testament name that was revived in the 17th
century by the Puritans. It is seldom used in
England, but is still found in North America.
Eph is a short form.

EPPIE see **EUPHEMIA**

ERASMUS *m.* (*eraz'mes*)

from the Greek, meaning 'beloved, desired',
and the name of an early Christian martyr.
The Dutch scholar and religious reformer Desi-
derius Erasmus (1465-1536) made the name
famous, although it was used in Britain before
his influence was exerted.

ERASTUS *m.* (*erast'es*)

from the Greek, meaning 'beloved, desired'.
The short form **Rastus** is better known in
Britain and in North America, but the name
is rare.

ERIC *m.*, ERICA *f.* (*e'rik, e'rike*)

from Norse; the second syllable means 'ruler';
the first is doubtful but possibly means 'ever'.
The name was brought to Britain about the
9th century by the Danes and its use has been
spasmodic ever since. Possibly Dean Farrar's
book *Eric or Little by Little* was largely responsible for its revival in the 19th century. It is
now very popular. Erica, the feminine form,
is now sometimes identified with the Latin
botanical name for heather. Both forms are
sometimes spelt with a 'k'. Short forms are

Rex and **Rickie** or **Rick**, and in North America, **Air** and **Erie**.

ERIN *f.* (*er'in, er'en*)

from the Gaelic Eireann, a poetical term for Ireland. It is a modern name, particularly popular in the U.S. and Australia.

ERMIN *see* EMLYN

ERMYNTRUDE *see* EMMA

ERNEST *m.*, ERNESTINE *f.* (*er'nist, ernistēn'*)

from the Old German, meaning 'vigour' or 'earnestness', it is sometimes spelt **Earnest**. It was introduced by the Hanoverians in the late 18th century and was common in the 19th century. Oscar Wilde's play, *The Importance of Being Earnest* (1899), increased its popularity. Ernestine, the feminine form, is, like Ernest, not very common today. Shortened forms are **Ern** and **Ernie**. The latter is the acronym nickname commonly used in Britain for Electronic Random Number Indicating Equipment, the premium bond prize selector.

ERROL m. (er'el)

It is not certain whether this name is a development of Eral, a medieval form of HAROLD or whether it is a variant of EARL. Errol Flynn, the film actor, was a well-known example who popularized the name. It may also be connected with the Irish word for 'pledge'.

ESMÉ f. (ez'mā)

probably from the French for 'esteemed' but treated as synonymous with the French Aimé, meaning 'beloved' (see AMY). It passed from France to Scotland and the Stuart family in the 16th century, and then to England but not until much later. It is now more often used as a girl's name.

ESMERALDA(H) f. (ezmeral'de)

Spanish for 'emerald'. It was used by the French 19th-century writer Victor Hugo for the heroine in his novel *The Hunchback of Notre Dame*, and has occasionally been used since in Britain and France. The English form **Emerald** is occasionally found.

ESMOND m. (ez'mend)

from the Old English compound of 'grace' or 'beauty' and 'protection'. The name was never common, and fell out of use in the 14th century. Its modern use probably dates from Thackeray's novel *The History of Henry Esmond* (1852). It is nowadays rather rare.

ESS, ESSIE, ESSY *see* ESTHER

ESTELLA *f.* (*estel'e*)

from the latin *stella* and the French *étoile*, meaning 'star'. It was a French name given by Charles Dickens to the heroine of *Great Expectations*, and has been used quite frequently since. **Estelle** is another form of the name. It sometimes shares the shortened forms of ESTHER (*see also* STELLA).

ESTHER, ESTER *f.* (*es'te*)

In the Old Testament the name is given as the Persian equivalent of a Hebrew word meaning 'myrtle'. It was interchangeable with **Hester** and appears in England in the 17th century, adopted by the Puritans. Racine's play *Esther* helped to popularize it in the 17th century, especially in France. Shortened forms include **Essy**, **Essie** and **Ess**.

ETHEL *f.* (*eth'el*)

This name was not originally independent. It arose in the 19th century as a shortening of various Anglo-Saxon names beginning with the root Ethel-, from the Old English *aethel*, meaning 'noble'. Its vogue in the 19th century was due to its use by popular authors like Thackeray. It has fallen out of favour in the 20th century.

ETHELBERT *m.* (*eth'elbet*)

from the Old English, meaning 'noble bright', and the name of a 6th-century Anglo-Saxon king. A convert to Christianity and the teachings of St Augustine, he was the first Archbishop of Canterbury. The name died out after the Norman Conquest, having only a brief revival in the 19th and 20th centuries.

ETHELMER *see* ELMER

ETHELRED *m.* (*e'thelred*)

from the Old English, meaning 'noble counsel', a fairly common Old English name. It probably died out after the Norman Conquest but was revived in the 19th century during a period in which Old English names were favoured.

ETHELREDA *see* AUDREY

ETHNE, EITHNE *see* AITHNE

ETTA, ETTIE *see* **ADA, HENRIETTA**

EUFEMIA *see* **EUPHEMIA**

EUGENE *m.*, **EUGENIA** *f.* (*ūjēn'*, *ūjēnēe*)

---

from the Greek, meaning 'well-born'. Its use in Britain and France was largely due to the fame of the 18th-century Prince Eugène of Savoy, the great general and ally of Marlborough. In North America the masculine form is usually abbreviated to **Gene**. Eugénie (*ūzhā'ni*), the French form, came into use from the French Empress Eugénie (1826-1920) who spent the last 50 years of her life in England.

EUGENIUS *see* **OWEN**

EUNICE *f.* (*ū'nis*)

---

from the Greek, meaning 'happy victory' or possibly 'wife'. The name is mentioned in the New Testament and was adopted by Puritans in the 17th century. It is still used today but not widely and is sometimes spelt **Unice**.

EUPHEMIA *f.* (*ūfē'mie*)

---

from the Greek, meaning 'fair speech' or, by implication, 'silence'. It occurs as **Eufemia** and

133

Eupheme from the 12th century. Later it became confined to Scotland, where it is still found, usually abbreviated to **Effie**, **Eppie** or occasionally **Fay**.

EUSTACE *m.*, EUSTACIA *f.* (*ū'stes, ūstā'sēe*)

from the Greek, meaning 'rich in corn' and hence 'fruitful' generally. Because of the two saints Eustachius, this name was in use in Britain before the Norman Conquest and was popular from the 12th to the 16th centuries. The Italian Renaissance physician Eustachio gave his name to the Eustachian tubes which connect the ear and throat. Eustacia, the feminine form, was also used in the 18th and 19th centuries but is now rare. A short form, STACEY (or **Stacy**), is now a name in its own right.

EVA *see* EVE

EVADNE *f.* (*evad'ni*)

This is a Greek name of uncertain meaning. It was used occasionally in the early part of the 20th century and has acquired a comic reputation because of the transvestite character Evadne Hinge.

EVAN *m. (ev'en)*

This is the Welsh form of JOHN. It is also an anglicized form of the Irish Eoghan, which became Evan and EWAN in Scotland. It dates from about 1500 and is still common in Wales.

EVANGELINE *f. (ivan'jelēn)*

from the Greek, meaning 'evangel', 'bringer of good tidings', and first introduced by Longfellow for his poem *Evangeline* (1847). It is used fairly often in North America and occasionally in Britain.

EVE, EVA *f. (ēv', ē've)*

from the Hebrew, meaning 'life', and in the Old Testament the name of the first woman. Eva is the Latin form, Eve the vernacular. It was in use in Britain even before the Reformation, when Old Testament names were not generally popular. In Ireland it was probably substituted for the earlier Gaelic **Aoiffe**, meaning 'pleasant'. It is still a common name in both forms. The pet form is **Evie**. **Evita** is the Spanish pet form.

EVELINE, EVELINA *f. (evelēn, evelēne)*

There are two possible sources for this name. It may derive from the Irish, meaning 'pleasant' (the commonest form of the name in Ireland being **Eveleen**), or from the Old German variant of the name **Avi**, which was brought to England by the Normans, and was the basis of many surnames like Evelyn and Eveling (*see* EVELYN). The surname Evelyn was almost certainly the major source of the use of Evelyn as a masculine, and later feminine, Christian name. It is often used to transliterate the Gaelic **Eibhilin**, meaning 'light'.

EVELYN *m. and f.* (ēv'lin, ēv'elin)

This name was used as a masculine personal name in Britain around the 17th century and was derived from the surname. Although well known in the 20th century through the author Evelyn Waugh, its use as a man's name has declined, and it is now more common as a woman's name. Waugh's first wife was also called Evelyn and friends referred to them as 'He-Evelyn' and 'She-Evelyn'.

EVERARD *m.* (ev'eràd)

from the Old German for 'boar' and 'hard'. This French form was brought to Britain by the Normans and was fairly common in England in the 12th and 13th centuries. It has been used occasionally since.

EVERILD *see* **AVERIL**

EVIE, EVITA *see* **EVE**

EWAN, EWEN *m.* (*ū'en*)

from the Irish **Eoghan**, meaning 'a youth'. It is probably equivalent to the Welsh OWEN.

EZEKIEL *m.* (*ezē'kiel*)

from the Hebrew, meaning 'may God strengthen'. It is the name of an Old Testament prophet, and was used from the 17th century in Britain. It is still current in North America, where **Zeke** is the usual abbreviation.

EZRA *m.* (*ez're*)

from the Hebrew, meaning 'help', the name of the author of one of the Old Testament books. It was adopted as a Christian name by Puritans in the 17th century. The name is no longer common. A well-known example in the 20th century is Ezra Pound the American poet.

F

FABIAN m. (fā'bien)

from the Latin family name Fabianus, possibly
meaning 'bean-grower'. There was a pope and
a St Fabian in the 3rd century, and there is a
record of the name being used by a sub-prior
of St Albans in the 13th century. There is little
other evidence of it until the 16th century, but
its use as a surname shows that it was known
previously. It has not been widely used since
then. The Roman general **Fabius**, known as
the 'delayer' for his tactics, was the inspiration
for the Fabian Society, a socialist society
founded in 1884. A rare feminine form, **Fabienne**, comes from the French **Fabien**.

FAGAN, FAGIN m. (fā'gen, fā'gin)

from Irish Gaelic, meaning 'little fiery one'.
This predominantly Irish name is perhaps best
known for Charles Dickens' character, Fagin,
in *Oliver Twist*.

FAITH f. (fāth)

one of the Christian virtues used as names after the Reformation. It was formerly used for both sexes, but is now a girl's name. FAY(E) is a short form.

FANNY see **FRANCES, MYFANWY**

FARQUHAR m. (fàꞌke̱)

from the Gaelic words meaning 'man' and 'friendly'. It was the name of one of the kings of Scotland and is still used in the Highlands.

FARRAND, FERRANT, FARREN see **FERDINAND**

FAWN f. (fawn)

the word for a young deer, used as a first name.

FAY(E) f. (fā)

from French, probably meaning 'fairy'. It is also an abbreviation of FAITH and EUPHEMIA.

FEARGUS see **FERGUS**

FELICE, FELIS see **FELIX**

FELICIA *see* **FELIX**

FELICITY *f. (felis'iti)*

from the Latin, meaning 'happiness', and, in the form **Felicitas**, the name of two saints. It was used by the Puritans in the 17th century and is fairly common today.

FELIX *m.*, **FELICIA** *f. (fe'lix, felisīe)*

from Latin, meaning 'happy', and the name of many saints and four popes. It was widely used in the Middle Ages and had a fairly strong hold in Ireland, where it transliterated the Irish **Phelim**. The feminine form, Felicia, has a long history of use and was also very popular in the Middle Ages. Variant forms were **Felice** and **Felis**.

FENELLA *f. (fenel'e)*

from the Irish words meaning 'white' and 'shoulder'. The name became known in Britain in the 19th century as a result of Sir Walter Scott's novel *Peveril of the Peak*. The actress Fenella Fielding is a well-known modern example. The Irish form of the name is **Finola** or **Fionnuala** *(finōl'a)*, which can be shortened to **Nola** or **Nuala**.

FERDINAND *m.* (*fer'dinend*)

from the Old German words meaning 'journey'
and 'venture'. The name was never popular in
Germany but was common in Spain, especially
in the forms **Fernando** and **Hernando**, and
in Italy as **Ferrante** and **Ferdinando**. It was
fairly popular in England and France in the
form **Ferrand**, which was the origin of the
surnames **Farrand**, **Farrant** and **Farren**.
The Italian form Ferdinando was used in
England in the 16th and 17th centuries,
especially among the gentry in the Midlands.
Short forms are **Ferd**, **Ferdie** and occasionally
Nandy.

FERGUS, FEARGUS *m.* (*fer'ges*)

from the Irish words for 'man' and 'choice', and
a fairly common first name in Scotland and
Ireland. It is also used in the North of England.
Fergie is a short form.

FERN *f.* (*fen*)

the plant name used as a first name.

FERNANDO *see* FERDINAND

FERRAND *see* FERDINAND

FERRANTE *see* **FERDINAND**

FINOLA *see* **FENELLA**

FIONA *f. (feō'n̲e̲)*
___
from Gaelic, meaning 'fair'. It was first used in the 19th century by William Sharp as a pen name (Fiona Macleod). It is a popular first name, especially in Scotland.

FLAVIA *f. (flāvēe)*
___
a Roman family name, which probably meant something like 'blond-haired'.

FLEUR *f. (fl̲e̲r)*
___
from French, meaning 'flower'. It was first used as a Christian name in the 20th century, in John Galsworthy's series of novels, *The Forsyte Saga*. The English form **Flower** is also found.

FLIP *see* **PHILIP**

FLO, FLOY *see* **FLORENCE**

FLORA *f. (flaw're̲)*
___
from Latin, meaning 'flower'. Flora was the Roman goddess of flowers and the spring. It is

now a fairly popular first name in Britain, especially in the Scottish Highlands. A famous holder of the name was Flora Macdonald, who played an important part in the escape of Bonnie Prince Charlie after the Battle of Culloden in 1746. Well known in the 20th century is the actress, Dame Flora Robson.

FLORENCE f. (flor'ens)

from the Latin name Florentius, used by the Romans for both males and females, and derived from the word meaning 'blooming'. In the Middle Ages, Florence was used as often for a man as for a woman, but it has since ceased to be used as a man's name. Florence Nightingale was named after the town in Italy, and her fame popularized the name in the 19th century. Abbreviated forms are **Florrie**, **Flossie**, **Floy** and **Flo**.

FLOWER see FLEUR

FLOYD see LLOYD

FRANCES f. (fràn'sis)

from the feminine form of the Italian **Francesco** (see FRANCIS). **Francesca**, also in regular use, was first used in Italy in the 13th century, and, at about the same time, **Françoise** began to appear in France. **Francine** is another French form. The name was not used in Britain until the 15th century, and it became popular with the English aristocracy at the time of the Tudors. It is now generally used throughout Britain, the short forms being **Fanny, Fran, Francie** and **Frankie**.

FRANCIS m. (frăn'sis)

from Latin, meaning 'Frenchman'. The name became popular in Europe in the 15th century because of St Francis of Assisi. The Italian word **Francesco** was in fact only the Saint's nickname, his Christian name being Giovanni. It was first used in Britain in the 15th century, and the fame of Francis Drake, a century later, made the name better known. **Fran** is a short form and FRANK is an abbreviation.

FRANK m. (frank)

from the Old German, denoting a member of the Frankish tribe who gave their name to France. The name also means 'free' (see FRANKLIN) and is commonly used as a pet form of FRANCIS.

FRANKLIN *m.* *(frank'lin)*

from Middle English, meaning 'free'. In medieval times a franklin was a man who owned land in his own right but was not noble. A famous modern example was Franklin D. Roosevelt, the 32nd U.S. President.

FRASER, FRAZER *m.* *(frāze)*

a Scottish surname of unknown meaning, increasingly found as a first name.

FRED, FREDDIE, FREDDY *see* **ALFRED, FREDERICK**

FREDA *see* **WINIFRED**

FREDERICK *m.*, **FREDERICA** *f.* *(fred'rik, frederē'ke)*

from the Old German meaning 'peaceful ruler'. The German form **Friedrich** was the name of several emperors and of King Frederick the Great of Prussia. Common abbreviations are **Fred**, **Freddie** and **Freddy**. The feminine form is Frederica, the German form of which (**Frederika**) gives us the name **Frieda**.

FREYA f. (frāe, frā'ye)

the name of the ancient Norse goddess of beauty, love and fertility, best known from the writer and traveller, Dame Freya Stark.

FULVIA f. (ful'vēe)

the feminine form of a noble Roman family name meaning 'tawny-haired', used as a first name.

G

GABRIEL *m.*, GABRIELLE *f.* (*gā'briel, gabriel'*)

from Hebrew, containing the elements 'God', 'man' and 'strength, and possibly implying the phrase 'strong man of God'. In St Luke's gospel it is the name of the archangel of the Annunciation. The name has been used infrequently since the Middle Ages. Gabrielle, the feminine form taken from the French, is much more common. The Italian is also used. A short form is **Gaby**; and **Abby** is sometimes used.

GAENOR *see* JEN(N)IFER

GAIL *f.* (*gāl*)

a pet form of ABIGAIL, widely used as a name in its own right. The spellings **Gale** and **Gayle** are also found.

GAIUS *see* CAIUS

GARETH m. (gar'eth)

from the Welsh, meaning 'gentle'. This name
was used by the 16th-century writer Malory
in his *Morte d'Arthur*, and later by Alfred
Tennyson, the 19th-century poet, in *Gareth
and Lynnette*. It was due to the latter that this
popular name was revived in this century.
GARTH and GAR(R)Y can be used as short forms.

GARFIELD m. (gà'fĕld)

a surname meaning 'spearfield' in Old English,
used as a first name, probably after J.A.
Garfield (1831-81), 20th president of the USA.
The cricketer Sir Garfield (Gary) Sobers is a
well-known holder of the name, and also shows
its short form.

GARNIER see WARNER

GARRET see GERARD

GAR(R)Y m. (garē)

While this very popular name can be used as
a short form of both GARETH and GARFIELD, its
use as an independent name owes much to the
film star Gary Cooper (1901-61). He was born

Frank James Cooper, and chose his stage name from the American town of Gary.

GARTH *see* GARETH

GASPAR, GASPAR(D) *see* JASPER

GASTON *m.* (gas'ton)

from French. The name was originally spelt Gascon and meant a man from Gascony. Today it is a common French Christian name, and it has been used occasionally in Britain also.

GAVIN *m.* (ga'vin)

The old Welsh Gwaichmai, meaning 'hawk of May', became in English Sir **Gawain**, King Arthur's famous nephew. This became Gauvin in French, and from France was adopted in Scotland as Gavin. Originally confined to Scotland, the name is now popular throughout the English-speaking world.

GAY(E) *f.* (gā)

This name is simply the adjective meaning happy and lively, and its use is recent.

GAYLE *see* GAIL

GAYNOR *see* **JEN(N)IFER**

GEMMA *f.* (*jem'e*)

is the Italian word for 'gem'. Its modern use is probably due in part to the Italian saint Gemma Galgani (1875-1903), canonized in 1940. For a long time a rare name, it has now become one of the most popular in the country. It is sometimes spelt **Jemma**.

GENE *see* EUGENE

GENEVIEVE *f.* (*jen'evēv*)

a French name from an Old German compound name meaning 'woman of the race'. It is found in Latin records as **Genovera** and **Genovova**. St Genevieve is the patron saint of Paris; she saved the city from the Huns in the 5th century by her cool thinking and courage, and the name is very popular in France. It has been used in Britain since the 19th century.

GEOFFREY, JEFFREY *m.* (*jef'ri*)

from the Old German Gaufrid, meaning 'district peace'. The name seems also to have assimilated the Old German Gisfrid, meaning 'pledge peace'. Geoffrey was popular between the 12th and 15th centuries in England resulting in many surnames e.g. Jeffries, Jeeves, Jepson. Two famous medieval Geoffreys were Chaucer, the father of English literature, and Geoffrey of Mommouth, the 12th-century historian. It fell from favour from the 15th to the 19th centuries, when it returned to fashion. **Geoff** and **Jeff** are common abbreviations.

GEORDIE *see* GEORGE

GEORGE m. *(jawj')*

from the Greek, meaning 'tiller of the soil' or 'farmer'. The famous St George is said to have been a Roman soldier who was martyred in Palestine in A.D. 303. In early Christian art many saints were represented as trampling on a dragon, as a symbol of good conquering evil. This may be the explanation of how the legend of St George and the dragon originated. He was described as the personification of chivalry in medieval writing. From 1349, when Edward III founded the Order of the Garter and put it under St George's patronage, the latter was regarded as the patron saint of England. Despite this, the name was never much used until the Hanoverian succession in 1714 brought a line of Georges to the throne. **Geordie** is a Scottish and North Country pet form which is used as a nickname for Northumbrians in general.

GEORGINA *f.* (*jawjēn'e*)

This is the most common feminine form of GEORGE. It was first used in Britain in the 18th century, when George became popular. The form then was **Georgiana**, which is still sometimes used. Other feminine forms of **George** are **Georgia**, **Georgette** and **Georgine**.

GER, GERRY *see* GERALD

GERAINT *m.* (*gerīnt', jerāint'*)

This is a Welsh name, a variant form of the Latin **Gerontius**, which is derived from the Greek word meaning 'old'. The 19th-century poet, Alfred Tennyson used the old Welsh story of *Geraint and Enid* in his *Idylls of the King*, and it was from this that the name's modern use has stemmed. Geraint Evans is a well-known modern operatic singer.

GERALD *m.* (*jer'eld*)

from the Old German, meaning 'spear rule'. It was used in England from the 11th to the 12th century and was probably introduced by the Normans. The name flourished in Ireland due to the influence of the Fitzgerald family, the powerful rulers of Kildare. It was probably from Ireland that the name returned to England in the late 19th century. Shortened forms are **Ger**, **Gerry** and **Jerry**.

GERALDINE *f.* (*jer'eldēn*)

There is no evidence of how this name arose, other than in the works of a 16th-century poet, praising the beauty of Lady Elizabeth Fitzgerald. Geraldine therefore means 'one of the Fitzgeralds'.

GERARD *m.* (*jer'ard*)

from the Old German, meaning 'spear hard'. It was brought to Britain by Norman settlers and was very common in the Middle Ages. The surnames Gerrard and Garrett are derived from it, and these were the most common medieval pronunciations of the Christian name. **Garret** is still used in Ireland, as in the case of the Irish statesman Garret Fitzgerald. **Gerry** and **Jerry** are used as short forms.

GERONIMUS *see* JEROME

GERONTIUS *see* GERAINT

GERTRUDE *f.* (*ger'trŏod*)

from the Old German, meaning 'spear strength'. The name came to Britain from the Netherlands, where a saint of that name was much venerated. It appears in many forms from the Middle Ages until the 19th century, when it was finalized as Gertrude, and became very popular. It is still in use, with the pet forms **Gert** or **Gertie** and **Trudie**.

GERVAIS, GERVASE *m.* (*jer'vāz*)

from the Old German, meaning 'spear vassal' or 'armour bearer'. The name was first used among English churchmen of the 12th century in honour of the 1st-century martyr St Gervase. It spread to the laity, giving rise to the surname Jarvis. Gervais is the French spelling.

GIB *see* GILBERT

GIDEON *m.* (*gid'ien*)

from Hebrew, now generally thought to mean 'having a stump for a hand', although the traditional translation was 'a hewer'. In the Old

Testament it is the name of the Israelite leader who routed the Midianites with three hundred men. The name was adopted at the Reformation and was a favourite among the Puritans, who took it to North America, where it is still in use.

GIGI *f.* (*zhēzhē*)

This name became well-known in 1958, when the novel *Gigi* by the French writer Colette was made into a very successful musical film. In the book Gigi is a pet form of Gilberte, the French feminine form of GILBERT.

GILBERT *m.* (*gil'bet*)

from the Old German meaning 'pledge bright'. The Normans brought the name to England and it was common in medieval times. The broadcaster Gilbert Harding made the name well-known in the 20th Century. Shortened forms are *Gib*, *Gilly*, *Bert* and *Bertie*.

GILES *m.* (*jīls*)

St Giles was an Athenian who took his name, Aegidius, from the goatskin that he wore. He left Greece in order to escape the fame of his miracles, and became a hermit in France.

There the name took root as *Gilles*, which possibly derived from Celtic *gille* or 'servant', because of his humility, rather than a derivative of Aegidius. The name is first recorded in England in the 12th century, but despite the large number of churches dedicated to this saint, the name was not popular. It has been suggested that this may be because of St Giles' association with beggars and cripples of whom he is the patron saint. However, recent years have seen a marked increase in its popularity. It is occasionally spelt *Gyles*.

GILL, GILLOT *see* **GILLIAN** (f.)

GILLEAN, GILLEON *see* **GILLIAN** (m.)

GILLES *see* **GILES**

GILLESPIE *see* **CELESTE**

GILLIAN f. (*jil'ien, gil'ien*)

This name, which is an English rendering of the Latin JULIAN, was so common in the Middle Ages that it was used as a general term for a girl, as Jack was for a man. The pet forms **Gill**, **Gillot** and **Gillet** were common, and from the last of these came the expression 'to jilt', which was why the name lost favour in the late 17th century. It was revived in the 20th century, and once more became very popular. A variant form is **Jillian**, and **Jill**, the abbreviated form, is now given as an independent name. **Jilly** is also found. The male form, also spelt **Gillean**, **Gilleon** and **Gillon**, is probably derived from the Gaelic Gill' Eoin, meaning servant of St John, and is found occasionally in the Scottish Highlands.

GILLIES *see* GILES

GINA *f.* (*jē'ne*)

a short form of such names as Georgina and Regina, now used as an independent name. The success of the Italian actress Gina Lollobrigida made it better known in this country.

GINNY *see* VIRGINIA

GISELLE *f.* (*jizel'*)

from the Old German meaning a 'pledge' or 'hostage'. **Gisèle** has for a long time been a common French name, and the English form **Giselle** and the latinized **Gisela** have been used in Britain.

GIULIA *see* **JULIA**

GIULIETTA *see* **JULIET**

GLADYS *f.* *(glad'is)*

This is the anglicized form of **Gwladys**, which is generally thought to be the Welsh equivalent of CLAUDIA. It may have had an earlier source, but this is now lost. It was first used in England in the late 19th century since when it has become widespread. In recent decades it has become less fashionable. It is often shortened to **Glad**.

GLEN(N), GLYN(N) *m.* *(glen, glin)*

are both forms of Celtic words for 'a valley'. In the last forty years both have become very popular names throughout the English-speaking world.

GLENDA *f.* *(glen'de)*

This is a Welsh name meaning 'holy-good'. The actress Glenda Jackson is a well-known user of the name.

GLENYS *f. (glen'is)*

from the Welsh meaning 'holy'. It is spelt in a variety of ways, including **Glenis**, **Glennys** and **Glenice** (*see* GLYNIS).

GLORIA *f. (glaw'rie)*

This is Latin for 'glory' or 'fame', and the name seems to have been coined by Bernard Shaw (1889) in his play *You Never Can Tell*. It was very common in the first half of the 20th century, although its popularity is now waning.

GLYNIS *f. (glin'is)*

is from the Welsh for 'a little valley'. It can be spelt **Glinys**, and is often confused with GLENYS.

GODFREY *m. (god'fri)*

from the Old German meaning 'God's peace'. There was an equivalent Old English name **Godfrith**, but Godfrey probably derives from the Norman form.

GORDON *m. (gaw'den)*

This was originally a Scottish place name, probably in Berwickshire from which the local lords took their name, founding a large and famous clan. It was rarely used as a Christian name until 1885, when the tragic death of General Gordon at Khartoum gave the name immense popularity.

GRACE f. (grās)

from Latin *gratia*, meaning 'grace', in its original religious sense. This name existed as Gracia in the Middle Ages but did not become common until the Puritans adopted it, along with the name of other Christian qualities. Its popularity waned in the 18th century, but it came back into favour when Grace Darling captured the hearts of the people with her heroic exploit in 1838. With her father, the lighthouse-keeper of the Farne Islands, she rescued nine survivors from a shipwreck in a terrifying storm. **Gracie**, though really a pet form, is sometimes given as a separate name. The singer and comedienne Gracie Fields made the name famous in Britain in the 20th century.

GRAHAM m. (grā'em)

Like Gordon, this was originally an English place name which developed into a family name, particularly on the English/Scottish border, and is now a very common name in Scotland. It gradually came into general use as a first name. The comedian **Graeme** Garden shows another form of the name, and **Grahame** is also found.

GRAINNE, GRANIA *f. (grone, gràne)*

possibly from the Irish, meaning 'loved', now anglicized as Grania, although GRACE and GERTRUDE have both been used. In Irish and Scottish legend, Grainne was the daughter of Cormac O'Coulin, Earl of Ulster, who betrothed her to Finn MacCoul, the famous chieftain. When she deserted Finn for Diarmid, the progenitor of the Clan Campbell, he hunted them down.

GRANT *m. (grànt)*

a surname from the French word meaning 'tall, large', used as a first name. It seems to have come to this country from the USA, where its introduction may have been connected with the popularity of General Ulysses Grant, 18th President.

GREGORY *m. (greg'eri)*

from the Greek, meaning 'watchman'. The name first came to Britain through St Gregory the Great, the Pope who sent St Augustine to England. It was in common use from the time of the Norman Conquest, when most Latin names were introduced, until the Reformation when, because of its association with the Papacy, it fell out of use. **Gregour** was the usual medieval form, which is still found as **Gregor** in Scotland, and hence the surname MacGregor. The most common shortened form is **Greg**.

GRETA *f.* (*grē'te*)

a Swedish abbreviation of MARGARET. It was rare in England until the 20th century, when the fame of the film actress Greta Garbo gave the name some vogue.

GRETEL, GRETCHEN *f.* (*gret'el, grech'en*)

the German diminutive form of MARGARET. These names are rarely used in Britain.

GRIFFITH *m.* (*grif'ith*)

from the Welsh name Gruffud, **Gruffydd** meaning 'lord', or 'strong warrior'. It has always been fairly popular in Wales, and was the name of several Welsh princes. It is not,

however, widely used throughout Britain.
Griff is a pet name.

GRISELDA, GRIZEL *f.* (*grizel'de, griz'el*)

from Old German, the meaning being disputed
but possibly 'grey battle-maiden'. Chaucer
gave rise to its use in Britain by including it
in his *Clerk's Tale*, the story of which he took
from Boccaccio. **Zelda** is a short form.

GRUFFUD, GRUFFYDD *see* GRIFFITH

GUARIN *see* WARREN

GUENDOLEN *see* GWENDOLYN

GUENEVERE *see* JEN(N)IFER

GUIDO *see* GUY

GUS, GUSSIE *see* AUGUSTUS

GUY *m.* (*gī*)

from the Old German **Wido**, the derivation of
which is uncertain. Wido became Guido in
Latin records and Guy was the French form
introduced to Britain by the Normans. Apparently the medieval clergy identified the name

with the Latin **Vitus** meaning 'lively', hence the disease St Vitus' Dance is known in France as *la danse de Saint Guy*. St Vitus was a Sicilian martyr who was invoked for the cure of nervous ailments. The name fell out of use after Guy Fawkes' gunpowder plot in the 17th century. It was revived in the 19th century with the help of Walter Scott's novel *Guy Mannering*.

GWEN(DA) *f. (gwen, gwen'de)*

from the pet form of several names, such as GWENDOLEN, which come from the Welsh word meaning 'white'. Gwen and Gwenda (an uncommon pet form) are now used as separate names and have spread to the rest of Britain.

GWENDOLYN, GWENDOLEN, GUENDOLEN *f. (gwen'dolin)*

from the Welsh meaning 'white circle', probably a reference to the ancient moon-goddess. The name occurs frequently in Welsh legend. Guendolen was the name of a fairy with whom King Arthur fell in love, and also of the wife of Merlin the magician.

GWILYM *see* WILLIAM

GWLADYS *see* **GLADYS**

GWYN *m. (gwin)*

from the Welsh meaning 'white' or 'blessed'.
This name has been anglicized as **Wyn** or
Wynne. It is most popular in Wales.

GWYNETH *f. (gwin'eth)*

from Welsh meaning 'blessed' or 'happy'. It
is quite a common name in Wales, and has
occasionally been used in England. **Gwyn** is
the pet form.

GYLES *see* **GILES**

H

HADRIAN *see* **ADRIAN**

HAL *see* **HENRY**

HALBERT *see* **ALBERT**

HALLAM *m.* (*hal'em*)

This is a surname which has been used as a
Christian name since 1850, when Tennyson
wrote his great elegy *In Memoriam* about his
gifted friend Arthur Henry Hallam, who had
died in 1843 aged only twenty-two. It is not a
very common name.

HAM *see* **ABRAHAM**

HAMISH *m.* (*hā'mish*)

the anglicized form of the Gaelic Seumas,
equivalent to JAMES. This name became popular in the second half of the 19th century, and
is still common in Scotland.

HANK *see* HENRY

HANNAH *f.* (han'e)

from the Hebrew, meaning 'He has favoured me'. In the Old Testatment it was the name of Samuel's mother. It was the Greek form ANNA which first became established throughout Europe. Hannah was only adopted in England after the Reformation.

HARIVIG *see* HARVEY

HAROLD *m.* (har'eld)

from the Old Norse, meaning 'army-power'. It was used in the Middle Ages, but went out of fashion until the 18th century when it became popular again. Its modern popularity stems from 19th-century literature celebrating King Harold II, the last of the Saxon Kings, who fought William the Conqueror, and was killed at Hastings in 1066. It shares the abbreviation **Harry** with HENRY.

HARRIET *f.* (har'iet)

a feminine form of HENRY, from Harry, which was its usual form in the Middle Ages. It was also spelt **Harriot**. The name was at the height of its popularity between the 18th and 19th centuries and has recently had a revival.

HARRISON m. (ha'ris_en)

a surname meaning 'son of Harry' used as a first name. It was popular in the last century. A modern user is the actor Harrison Ford.

HARRY see HAROLD, HENRY

HARTLEY m. (hāt'li)

This surname was taken from a common place name derived from the Old English meaning 'deer pasture'. It is now quite often used as a Christian name.

HARUN, HAROUN see AARON

HARVEY m. (hà'vi)

from the French, meaning 'battleworthy'. It may also have been used to transliterate the Saxon Harivig, after the Norman Conquest. It remained common until the 14th century, and had a slight revival in the 19th. Its modern use as a Christian name may be due in part to its widespread use as a surname.

HATTIE, HATTY *see* **HARRIET**

HAVELOCK *see* **OLIVER**

HAYDEN, HAYDON, HAYDN *see* **AIDAN**

HAYLEY *f.* (hā'lē)

from the surname, meaning 'hay field'. This name came into use in the 1960s, after the success of the film actress Hayley Mills, and has since become very popular.

HAZEL *f.* (hā'zel)

This is one of several plant names adopted as a girl's name in the 19th century.

HEATHER *f.* (heTH'e)

This is one of the plant names first used as a first name in the 19th century, and one of the more common ones today, especially in Scotland.

HECTOR *m.* (hek'te)

from the Greek, meaning 'hold fast'. It was the name of the Trojan hero who was killed by the Greek Achilles. 'Sir **Ector**' became a hero of popular literature in the Middle Ages, and it was from this that the general use of the name arose. It took a strong hold in Scotland, where it was used as an equivalent for the quite unconnected Gaelic name **Eachan**, meaning 'a horseman'.

HELEN *f.* (*hel'en*)

from the Greek, meaning 'the bright one'. The popularity of this name in Britain was due originally to the 4th-century St **Helena**. She was the mother of Constantine the Great and was supposed to have been the daughter of the Prince of Colchester, the Old King Cole of nursery rhyme. When she was over eighty she made a pilgrimage to the Holy Land where she was believed to have found the true cross of Christ. The name is first found as **Elena** and then ELAINE and **Ellen**. The 'h' was not used until the Renaissance, when the study of classical literature brought Homer's story of the Trojan war and the beautiful Greek queen Helen to public notice. **Lena** is a contraction of Helena (*see* ELEANOR).

HELGA *f.* (*hel'ge*)

from the Norse, meaning 'holy'. It has occasionally been used in Britain but is more common in North America, where it was introduced by Scandinavian immigrants (*see* OLGA).

HENRI, HENRICUS *see* HENRY

HENRIETTA *f.* (*henriet'e*)

the feminine form of HENRY. It was introduced into this country in the 17th century by **Henriette** Marie, Charles I's French wife. The full form gave way to the abbreviated HARRIET, but was revived in the 19th century. Abbreviations are **Etta**, **Ettie** and **Hetty**.

HENRY *m.* (*hen'ri*)

from the Old German, meaning 'home ruler'. The Latin **Henricus** became **Henri** in France. **Harry** was, in fact, the original English form of Henri, used until the 17th century and often abbreviated to **Hal**. Today Harry is used as the pet form of Henry. **Hank** is a pet form more common in America.

HERBERT *m.* (*her'bet*)

from the Old German, meaning 'bright army'. It seldom appears before the Norman Conquest, after which it was reintroduced and became quite common. It was revived at the beginning of the 19th century, and became popular again towards the end of the century. This latest revival was partly due to the fashion for adapting aristocratic surnames, but has also been attributed to the popularity of George Herbert's hymns. **Herb, Herbie** and **Bert** or **Bertie** are short forms.

HERMIONE *f.* (*hermĭ'oni*)

from the Greek, meaning 'daughter of Hermes' and in Greek mythology, the daughter of Menelaus and Helen. It was Shakespeare's use of the name in *A Winter's Tale* that gave rise to its use in modern times. He used another form, **Hermia**, in *A Midsummer Night's Dream*, and this also has been used from time to time.

HERNANDO *see* FERDINAND

HESTER *see* ESTHER

HETTY *see* HENRIETTA

HEW *see* HUGH

HIERONYMOS *see* JEROME

HILARY, HILLARY *m. and f. (hil'eri)*

from the Latin, meaning 'cheerful'. The name was popular in France due to the influence of St Hilarius, a strong supporter of Christianity in the 4th century. It came to England in the Middle Ages and has been used occasionally ever since. It is more common now as a girl's name.

HILDA *f. (hil'de)*

from the Old English, meaning 'battle'. There was an Anglo-Saxon St Hilda who founded an abbey at Whitby in the 7th century. When the names of Anglo-Saxon saints were revived in the 19th century, Hilda became popular, and it is still in common use throughout Britain.

HIRAM *m. (hī'rem)*

from the Hebrew, meaning 'brother' and 'high' or 'exalted', and the name of a king of Tyre in the Old Testament. It was a favourite name in the 17th century and was taken at that time to North America where the name still flourishes.

HODGE *see* **ROGER**

HOLLY f. (ho'lē)

the plant name used as a first name. It has become a very popular name in recent years. Holly Martins, the hero of Graham Greene's *The Third Man*, is a rare example of its use as a man's name.

HONOR(I)(A) f. (on'e, onaw're, onaw'rie, honaw'rie)

from the Latin, meaning 'reputation' or 'honour'. The Latin forms Honora, Honoria and **Annora** were predominant till the Reformation, when the Puritans adopted abstract virtue names and used **Honour** and Honor. They were then used both as masculine and feminine names. In the 19th century the Latin forms came back briefly. At the moment Honor is most popular, and it is an exclusively feminine name.

HONORIUS see **ANEURIN**

HONOUR see **HONOR**

HOPE f. (hōp)

This Christian quality was adopted as a first name in the 17th century, like Honour, Faith,

Charity, etc. It was especially popular among Puritans at this time, who used it for both sexes, but it is now thought of as a female name.

HORACE, HORATIO m. (hor'_es_, horā'shio)

from the Latin clan named Horatius, of which the famous Roman soldier, **Horatius** Cocles, was a member. The fame of the name is also due to the Latin poet Horace who adopted it. Horatio seems to have come from Italy to England in the 16th century. Horace is the form which is most often used today, though the 1st Viscount Nelson made the Horatio form well-known. **Horatia** is a rare feminine form.

HOWARD m. (how'_ed_)

Like other aristocratic family names this was adopted as a first name by the general public in the 19th century. The origin of the surname is disputed. It may be from Old German meaning 'heart-protection' or the French for 'worker with a hoe', or even from the medieval official the 'Hogwarden' who superintended the pigs of a district.

HUBERT m. (hū'bet)

from the Old German, meaning 'heart bright'.
This name was very popular in the Middle
Ages, probably as a result of the fame of St
Hubert of Liège, the patron saint of huntsmen.
It was not used from the 15th-19th centuries,
after which it was revived to some extent, but
it has since gone out of fashion again.

HUGH, HUGO m. (hū', hū'gō)

from the Old German, meaning 'heart' or 'soul'.
It was brought to Britain by the Normans and
appears frequently in the Domesday Book. It
was further strengthened by the popularity of
St Hugh, Bishop of Lincoln in the 14th century.
Hugo is the Latin form, and both are still quite
common, Hugh being used as a transliteration
of certain Gaelic names in Scotland and
Ireland. **Hew** and **Huw** are Welsh forms of
the name. **Hughie** and **Huey** are used as pet
forms.

HUMPHREY m. (hum'fri)

from the Old English, meaning 'giant peace'.
This name was originally spelt with an 'f', the
'ph' coming in when it was equated with the
name of the Egyptian St Onuphrios in order

to Christianize it. The name appears in the Old English period, and its popularity was reinforced by the Norman Conquest. At first it was confined to the nobility, but later its use became general. As a result of becoming too common, it fell out of favour but was revived in the 19th century.

HUNTER m. (hun'te)

from Old English for 'a hunter'. This is sometimes used as a first name, possibly in connection with the surname, which is far more common. The writer, Hunter Davies, is a well-known example.

HYWEL m. (how'el)

a Welsh name meaning 'eminent'. It has become well known through the actor Hywel Bennett.

I

IAN, IAIN *see* **JOHN**

IDA *f.* (*ī'de*)

from the Old German, meaning 'hard work'.
The name was introduced by the Normans,
and lasted until about the middle of the 14th
century. It was the name of the heroine of
Tennyson's poem *The Princess* (1874), and Gilbert and Sullivan's opera *Princess Ida* (1884),
based on it, led to a revival of the name at the
end of the 19th century.

IDRIS *m.* (*id'ris*)

This is a Welsh name meaning 'fiery lord'. In
Welsh legend Idris the Giant was an astron-
omer and magician, who had his observatory
on Cader Idris.

IEUAN *see* **JOHN**

IFOR *see* **IVOR**

IGNATIUS *m.* (*ignā'shes*)

This is a Latin name, derived originally from a Greek name of obscure origin. It occasionally takes the form INIGO.

ILONA *f.* (*ilō'ne*)

This is a rare name derived from the Hungarian meaning 'beautiful one'. It has been suggested that it is a variant form of HELEN.

ILSABETH *see* ISABEL

IMOGEN *f.* (*im'ojen*)

First appearing in Shakespeare's *Cymbeline*, this name is thought to be a misprint of the **Innogen** which appears in Holinshed, Shakespeare's source for the story. The medieval historian Geoffrey of Monmouth also uses the name, but its etymology is uncertain. It may be derived from the Greek meaning 'beloved child'. The composer and conductor Imogen Holst is a well-known modern example of the name.

INA *f.* (*ē'ne*)

This name can come from three different sources. It is an Irish form of AGNES, a form of the name ENA, and can also be a pet form of first names ending '-ina', such as Christina and Georgina.

INDIA f. (in'dēe)

the name of the country used as a first name. It was not used before this century.

INES, INEZ see AGNES

INGRID f. (ing'rid)

from the Old Norse, meaning 'Ing's ride'. Ing in Norse mythology was the god of fertility and crops, and his steed was a golden bristled boar. The name is common in Scandinavia. The Swedish film star Ingrid Bergman (1915–82) made the name famous and popular in this country.

INIGO m. (in'igō)

from Greek but of obscure meaning, possibly meaning 'fiery'. The 1st-century Bishop of Antioch of this name was by tradition the author of the Epistles to the Romans and Ephesians. The name took root mainly in Russia and Spain. It was carried further afield by the Jesuits whose founder was Inigo Lopez de

Recalde or St IGNATIUS de Loyola, as he was popularly known. The best known holder of the name in Britain was Inigo Jones, the 17th-century architect.

INNOGEN see IMOGEN

IOLA f. (ī′ōle)

from the Greek, meaning 'dawn cloud'. In Greek mythology Hercules fell in love with a princess Iole and captured her. The name is rare in Britain.

IOLANTHE see YOLANDE

IONA f. (īō′ne)

from the Greek, meaning 'violet coloured stone'. In Scotland the name is usually taken from the name of the Hebridean island. Ione is also used.

IOR see IVOR

IRA m. (īre)

a name from the Old Testament meaning 'watchful'. The name was used by the Puritans, who took it over to America where it is now much more common than in Britain. The song writer Ira Gershwin is a famous bearer of the name.

IRENE f. (īrēn', īrē'ni)

from the Greek, meaning 'peace', and the name of the goddess of peace in ancient Greece. Although the name was used earlier in other parts of Europe, it was not used in England until the late 19th century. It is now very common. The original pronunciation was īrē'ni, but the American īrēn' is now more popular in Britain also. The abbreviation **Renie** is sometimes used.

IRIS f. (ī'ris)

Although this name is usually associated with the flower, it comes from the Greek word for 'rainbow', after which the flower was named, because of its bright colours. In Greek mythology Iris carried messages from the gods to men, across the rainbow which was her bridge. It was not used in England before the 19th century.

IRMA f. (e'me)

This was originally a German name meaning 'universal'. It has only been used in this country since the end of the last century (*see* EMMA).

IRVIN(G) *m.* (*er'vin(g)*)

The origin of this name is disputed. It is either from Old English Earwine, meaning 'sea friend' or Old Welsh Erwyn, meaning 'white river'. The modern use of the name may have been influenced by its use as a surname. Modern examples are Irving Berlin (b. 1888), the composer, and Irving Stone (b. 1903), the author.

ISA *see* ISABEL

ISAAC, IZAAK *m.* (*ī'zek*)

from the Hebrew, meaning 'laughter'. It was the name given by Sarah, wife of Abraham, to the son born in her old age. The name is popularly believed to have been chosen by Sarah because she laughed when she was told that she would conceive. The name appears in Britain in the Middle Ages, but it came to be regarded as a specifically Jewish name. The name came into general use in the 16th and 17th centuries, when it was spelt with a 'z' as in Izaak Walton, the author of *The Compleat Angler*. In the mid-17th century the 's' spelling came into vogue, as in Sir Isaac Newton, the great scientist. **Zak** is occasionally used as a pet form, but **Ike** is more common. Modern uses of Ike can also refer to President Dwight D. Eisenhower (1890-1969) who was nicknamed Ike.

ISABEL(LA), ISOBEL f. (izebel'(e), iz'obel)

These variants of ELIZABETH seem to have originated in medieval France. Elizabeth became **Ilsabeth** and then **Isabeau**, and finally **Isabelle**. Up to the end of the 17th century at least, the derivatives **Isabel(le)** in England, Isobel in Scotland and the Gaelic **Iseabail**, sometimes transliterated as **Ishbel**, were interchangeable with Elizabeth. ISA and Bel(le) were the common short forms, and the latinized **Isabella** and **Bella** were used from the 18th century.

ISAIAH m. (īzī'e)

from the Hebrew, meaning 'Jehovah is generous', and the name of the great Old Testament prophet. It was first used by the 17th-century Puritans, and is rather rare today in Britain, although slightly more common in North America. The philosopher Sir Isaiah Berlin is a famous modern holder of the name.

ISEABAIL *see* **ISABEL**

ISEULT *see* **ISOLDA**

ISHBEL *see* **ISABEL**

ISIDORE *m.*, **ISIDORA** *f.* (*iz'edaw, izedaw're*)

from the Greek, possibly meaning 'gift of Isis'. The name was not common in ancient Greece. There were two Spanish saints of this name. The scandal caused by the private life and dancing style of Isadora Duncan (1878-1927) made the feminine form of the name well known.

ISLA *f.* (*i'le*)

the name of two Scottish rivers and used as a girl's name in Scotland since the 1950s. It has now spread to other parts of the country, the television appearances of Isla St Clair helping to make the name better known.

ISOLDA *f.* (*izōl'de*)

possibly from Old Welsh Essylt, meaning 'fair one', or Old German Isvald, meaning 'ice rule'. It was a common name in medieval times because of its place in Arthurian legend. **Iseult** was the Norman form which became Isolda in Latin, **Isot**(t) in Middle English. Isolda had a brief revival in the 19th century owing to the popularity of Wagner's opera *Tristan and Isolde*. It is also spelt **Yseult**(e) and **Ysolde**.

ISRAEL f. (*iz'rāl*)

from the Hebrew. The meaning is disputed but the most likely translation is 'may God prevail'. In the Old Testament Jacob was named Israel because of his struggle with the angel of God. The name was first adopted by Christians after the Reformation. It continued in use, mostly among the poorer classes, until the late 19th century, but is now uncommon.

IVAN m. (*īv'en, ēvan'*)

the Russian form of JOHN, occasionally found in Britain.

IVO m. (*ī'vō*)

from the Old German meaning 'yew'. It was common in Brittany in the form **Yves**, and was brought to Britain at the time of the Norman Conquest. It has been used very occasionally since.

IVOR, IFOR *m.* (ɪ'v_e_, ē'faw)

Ifor is a Welsh name which means 'lord', and Ivor is the anglicized spelling. It was originally **Ior**, but was probably influenced by the similar Breton **Yves**, which became IVO and was brought over by the Normans in this form.

IVY *f.* (ī'vi)

This is a plant name coined in the 19th century, which, perhaps because of its capacity for clinging, may signify faithfulness.

J

JACK *m.* (*jak*)

Originally the pet form of JOHN this is now a well-known independent name. It was formed from the Flemish diminutive Jankins, from which the 'n' was omitted in Britain. It was so common in the Middle Ages that it became a synonym for a man, and most of the popular uses of the word are derived from this. **Jock** is a variant used as an archetypal nickname for a Scotsman, but rarely given as a first name in Scotland. It has the pet form **Jake**, now a name in its own right.

JACKIE, JACKY, JACQUI *see* JACQUELINE

JACOB *m.* (*jā'keb*)

Originally Hebrew, the meaning of this name is uncertain. In the Old Testament it was the name of Isaac's younger son, who tricked his brother, Esau, out of his inheritance. This

explains the popular interpretation of the
name as 'he supplanted'. There were two Latin
forms, **Jacobus** and **Jacomus**. Jacob came
from the former and JAMES from the latter.
Jacob has survived as a Christian name
because the translators of the Bible kept this
form for the Old Testament Patriarch, although
they called the two New Testament apostles
James. Jacob was common after the Reformation, but in modern times has not enjoyed
anything like the popularity of James. **Jacoba**
and **Jacobina** are rare feminine forms. **Jake**
is an abbreviation used as a name in its own
right.

JACQUELINE, JACQUETTA *f.* (*jak'elin, jaket'e*)

These are French feminine diminutives of **Jac-
ques**, the French equivalent of JAMES and
JACOB. Both were introduced into this country
from Belgium in the 13th century, and have
been in use ever since. Jacqueline, with the
pet forms **Jacky**, **Jackie** or **Jacqui**, is the
more popular of the two today. It is found in a
very wide range of spellings which include
Jackalyn, **Jacaline**, **Jacquelyn** and
Jaqueline.

JADE *f.* (*jād*)

the precious stone used as a first name. Although the names of precious stones have been in use as girls' names since the last century, this one seems only to have come into use in the 1970s.

JAGO *see* JAMES

JAKE *see* JACK, JACOB, JESSE

JAMES *m.* (*jāmz*)

This name has the same root as JACOB. It became established in Britain in the 12th century, when pilgrims started to visit the shrine of St James, the son of Zebedee, at Compostella in Spain. At that time the name was more common in Scotland. With the accession of James as the first king of both England and Scotland, the name began to increase in popularity in England, in the 17th century. It was unfashionable in the 19th century, when it was used as a general term for a man servant, but is now more popular than ever. The pet forms are **Jim** and **Jimmy**, and in Scotland JAMIE is also used. The Irish form is **Seumas** or SHAMUS. The Cornish form **Jago** has recently become fashionable (*see also* HAMISH).

JAMIE *m. and f.* (*jāmē*)

this pet form of JAMES was originally a Scottish form but has since spread throughout the English-speaking world and become popular as a name in its own right. Since the 1960s it has also been used as a girl's name, particularly in the United States. It is also found in the form **Jaime**.

JAN *m. and f.* (*jan*)

The male form is a variant of JOHN originating in the West Country. Its use has now spread into other parts of Britain. It is also a form of John in a number of European languages such as Dutch and Polish and is then pronounced *yan*. The female version is a common pet form of JANET.

JANE *f.* (*jān*)

This is now the commonest feminine form of JOHN. It is derived from the Old French form **Jehane**. It was very rare before the 16th century, the medieval feminine forms of John being JOAN and JOANNA. An early example was Jane Seymour, Henry VIII's third wife, and mother of Edward VI. Since Tudor times the name has been in and out of fashion, until, in

associated it more with the Greek hero Jason (of the Argonauts) who won the Golden Fleece, rather than with the Bible.

JASPER, CASPAR m. (jas'pe, kas'pe)

Gaspar or Caspar was believed to have been the name of one of the three kings or 'wise men' of the Christmas story. His name may mean 'keeper' or 'bringer of treasure'. Gaspard is the French form and Jasper the English. Both names are still used, though the use of Jasper as a conventional name for a stage villain made it less popular for a time. The comedian Jasper Carrott and the fashion designer Jasper Conran have brought it back to public attention.

JAY m. and f. (ja)

This name derives most probably from a short form of any name beginning with a J, but it could also be a nickname from the bird and the noise it makes, indicating that the holder was a chatterer. It is sometimes spelt Jaye.

JAYNE see JANE

JEAN f. (jēn)

a Scottish form of JANE or JOAN derived from the Old French Jehane. It is a very popular name throughout Britain. The diminutive **Jeanette** is also found (*see* JANET). The commonest pet forms are **Jeanie** and **Jenny**.

JEANETTE *see* JANET, JEAN

JED *m.* (*jed*)

a short form of the Biblical name **Jedidiah**, 'beloved of the Lord', used as a name in its own right. It is much more common in the United States than in this country.

JEFF *see* GEOFFREY, JEFFREY

JEHANE *see* JANE

JEM *see* JEREMY

JEMIMA *f.* (*jemī'me*)

from the Hebrew, meaning 'dove', and the name of one of Job's daughters in the Old Testament. It was first used in the 17th century by Puritans, and was very popular in the 19th century. It may have been used as a feminine form of JAMES.

JEMMA *see* GEMMA

JEN(N)IFER f. (jen'ife)

Jennifer was an old Cornish form of **Guine-vere**, from the Welsh meaning 'fair and yield-ing', which was the name of King Arthur's wife. It was practically obsolete when it was revived in the 20th century. It spread rapidly, and is now very popular throughout Britain. **Jenny** or **Jenni** is the pet form. **Gaenor** and **Gaynor** are other forms of Guenevere, which is also spelt **Guinevere** and, in Wales, **Gwenhwyfar**. **Jenna**, another Cornish ver-sion of the name, has recently become very popular, no doubt helped by its use for a character in the television series *Dallas*.

JENNY *see* JANE, JEAN, JÉNNIFER

JEREMY, JEREMIAH m. (jer'emi, jeremīe)

from the Hebrew, meaning 'may Jehovah exalt'. Jeremiah was the Old Testament prophet who wrote the *Book of Lamentations*. The traditional English form is Jeremy, which appears from the 13th century onwards, and is very popular at present. In the 17th century the two forms **Jeremias** and **Jeremiah** were common. **Jerry** is the short form, which is shared with GERALD, and **Jem** is also used.

JEROME *m.* (*jerōm'*)

from the Greek **Hieronymos**, meaning 'holy name'. This name is pre-Christian in origin, but soon became popular with the early Church because of its association with the Lord's Prayer. St Jerome, who bore the Latin form **Hieronymus**, translated the Bible into Latin in the 4th century, and was an important religious influence in the Middle Ages. The name appears in England in the 12th century as **Geronimus**, which gradually gave way to the French form **Jérôme**. Famous holders of the name include Jerome K. Jerome who wrote *Three Men in a Boat* (1889) and the composer Jerome Kern.

JERRY *see* **JEREMY, GERALD, GERARD**

JESSAMINE, JESSAMYN *see* **JASMINE**

JESSE *f.* (*jes'i*)

from the Hebrew, meaning 'God exists', and, in the Old Testament, the name of King David's father. It was adopted in the 17th century by the Puritans, who took it to America, where it has been commoner than in this country. Jesse James, the mid-19th century American outlaw, and the politician Jesse Jackson are probably the best known examples. **Jess** is a short form, and **Jake** a pet form shared with JACOB. The name is sometimes spelt **Jessie**.

JESSICA f. (*jes'ik̲e̲*)

from the Hebrew, meaning 'God beholds'. Its use in Britain is probably due to the influence of Shakespeare's play, *The Merchant of Venice*, in which Shylock's daughter is called Jessica. It is shortened to **Jesse** or **Jessie**, sometimes spelt **Jessye**.

JESSIE f. (*jes'i̲*)

This is a Scottish diminutive of JANET but it is often used as a separate name. It is fairly common in the literature of the 18th and 19th centuries, and is also a pet form of JESSICA.

JETHRO m. (*jeth'rō*)

from the Hebrew, meaning 'abundance' or 'excellence'. It has occasionally been used as a first name since the Reformation. A well-known example is Jethro Tull, the 18th-century agricultural reformer whose name has been used recently by a successful pop group.

JHONE see JOAN

JILL f. (*jil*)

a pet form of Jillian or GILLIAN, often given as a separate name.

JILLIAN, JILLY *see* **GILLIAN, JULIANA**

JIM, JIMMY *see* **JAMES**

JO, JOE *see* **JOSEPH, JOSEPHINE**

JOAN f. (*jōn*)

This is the oldest English feminine form of JOHN and is a contraction of **Johanna**, the Latin feminine form of **Johannes**. The name came over from France as **Jhone** and **Johan** in the second half of the 12th century, but by the 14th century Joan was the established form. By the mid-16th century it was so common that it became unfashionable, and JANE superseded it. It was revived at the beginning of the 20th century, and is again very popular (*see* JOANNA). **Joni** is a pet form.

JOANNA, JOANNE f. (*jōan'e, jōan*)

Johanna was the medieval Latin feminine form of Johannes (*see* JOHN). Both it and **Johanna**, which is how it is rendered in the

Authorised Version of the New Testament (Luke XXIV, 20), were adopted in the 18th century. Joanna has been revived in the 20th century, and is once again a popular name. **Juanita** is the Spanish diminutive, which, with its short form **Nita** is also found in Britain.

JOB m. (jōb)

from the Hebrew, meaning 'hated' or 'persecuted'. The medieval use of the name may have had an Old German origin, but it was certainly used in its Biblical context after the Reformation. **Jobey**, **Jobie** or **Joby** are other forms of the name.

JOCELYN, JO(S)CELIN m. and f. (jos'(e)lin)

probably from the Latin, meaning 'cheerful', 'sportive'. There is also a possibility that it is derived from an old German name meaning 'little Goth'. A further derivation has been traced from the name **Josse**, 'champion', a form of **Jodoc**, the name of an early Breton saint.

JOCK see JACK, JOHN

JODIE, JODY *see* **JUDITH**

JODOC *see* **JOCELYN**

JODOCUS *see* **JOYCE**

JOEL *m.* (*jō'el*)

from the Hebrew, meaning 'Jehovah is God', and the name of one of the minor Old Testament prophets. It was adopted by Puritans, like many other Biblical names, after the Reformation.

JOHAN *see* **JOAN, JOHN**

JOHANE *see* **JEAN**

JOHANNA *see* **JOANNA**

JOHN *m.* (*jon*)

from the Hebrew, meaning 'the Lord is gracious' or 'Grace of the Lord'. This name was a favourite in the Eastern Church. The Crusaders brought it back to England, where it began to spread in the 12th century. Its earliest form in Europe was the Latin Johannes, which was shortened to **Johan** and Jon, and hence John. A particularly Scottish variant form is **Jock** (*see* JACK). **Ian** and **Iain** are the Gaelic forms, **Ieuan** and EVAN the Welsh, and SEAN or **Shane** the Irish. From the 16th century onwards, John became predominant as a boy's name, and it is still one of the commonest boys' names in Britain.

JOISSE *see* **JOYCE**

JOLYON *see* **JULIAN**

JON *see* **JOHN, JONATHAN**

JONAH, JONAS m. (*jō′ne, jō′nes*)

from the Hebrew, meaning 'dove'. The story of Jonah and the whale in the Old Testament was very popular in the Middle Ages and, because of this, the name was common. It was revived after the Reformation, and was used occasionally until the 19th century, when it died out, probably because of the association of the name with bad luck. Jonas was the Greek form and is now the more common of the two.

JONATHAN m. (*jon′ethen*)

from the Hebrew, meaning 'the Lord has given'. In the Old Testament, Jonathan was the son of King Saul and it was his great friendship with David that gave rise to the expression 'David and Jonathan' to describe two close friends. The name was taken into use at the time of the Reformation, and it is very popular today. The short form **Jon** is often used as a separate name.

JONI *see* **JOAN**

JOSCELIN *see* **JOCELYN**

JOSEPH *m.* (*jō'zef, jō'sef*)

from the Hebrew, meaning 'the Lord added' (i.e. to the family). In the Old Testament it was the name of Jacob and Rachel's elder son who was sold into slavery in Egypt. In the New Testament, there were Joseph, the husband of Mary, and Joseph of Arimathea, who is believed to have buried Jesus, and whom legend connects with Glastonbury and the Holy Grail. The name was not frequently used until the 17th century, when Old Testament names were adopted by the Puritans, and Joseph became a favourite. **Joe** and **Jo** are common abbreviations, and **Jos** is also found.

JOSEPHINE *f.* (*jō'zĕfĕn, jō'sĕfĕn*)

This was originally a pet form of **Josephe**, the French form of Josepha, which is the feminine of the Latin Josephus (*see* JOSEPH). It was Napoleon's first wife, the Empress Josephine, who started the fashion for the name in Britain and France. **Josepha** was also used in the 19th century. Pet forms are **Jo(e)** and **Josie**.

JOSHUA *m.* (*josh'ūe*)

from the Hebrew, meaning 'the Lord is generous'. In the Old Testament Joshua succeded Moses and finally led the Israelites to the Promised Land. The name was not used in England before the Reformation. Its most famous British bearer was Sir Joshua Reynolds, the painter, who was appointed the first President of the Royal Academy by George III. **Josh** is a popular short form.

JOSIAH *m.* (*jōzī'e*)

from the Hebrew, meaning 'may the Lord heal'. It was most common in the 17th century. The famous 18th-century potter, Josiah Wedgwood, in whose family the name is still used, is possibly the best known British bearer the name. **Josias** is an alternative form of the word, and **Jos** a short form.

JOSIE *see* JOSEPHINE

JOSSE *see* JOCELYN, JOYCE

JOY *f.* (*joi*)

This is just the word 'joy', taken from Latin, used as a Christian name. It occurs as early as the 12th century, and was revived in the 19th century.

JOYCE *m. and f.* (*jois*)

In the Middle Ages, when this name was most common, it usually had the form **Josse**. A 7th-century saint from Brittany, whose name was latinized to **Jodocus**, was the cause of the name's popularity. One of the French variants of the name was **Joisse**, and it was from this that the final form of the name was derived. The name was little used after the Middle Ages until the general revival of medieval names in the last century. It is now very rare as a man's name, although the author Joyce Cary (1888-1959) is one example.

JUANITA *see* JOANNA

JUDAS *see* JUDE

JUDE *m.* (jōōd)

The Hebrew form of this name is **Yehudi**, which was rendered as **Judah** in the Authorised Version of the Old Testament. **Judas** Iscariot bore the Greek form, and because of him the name was never used by Christians until the Reformation. Jude was used in the Authorised Version to distinguish the author of *The Epistle of Jude*. The name has been used occasionally, and is best known through Thomas Hardy's novel *Jude the Obscure* and the Beatles' song *Hey Jude*.

JUDITH *f.* (jōō'dith)

from the Hebrew, meaning 'a Jewess', and, in the Old Testament, the name of Esau's wife. The name appears both before and after the Norman Conquest, but did not become common until the 17th century. The short-form **Judy** is often given independently, as are the pet forms **Jody** or **Jodi(e)**.

JUHEL *see* JOEL

JULIA, JULIE *f.* (jōō'lie, jōō'li)

Julia is the feminine form of JULIUS, which came to England from Italy as Giulia in the

16th century, and was used by Shakespeare in *Two Gentleman of Verona*. It did not become common in Britain until the 18th and 19th centuries. **Julie**, the pet form taken from the French, is now more common as a given name than Julia (*see* JULIANA, JULIET).

JULIAN *m.* (*jŏŏ'lien*)

Latin **Julianus**, derived from JULIUS. The most famous of numerous saints of this name was St Julian the Hospitaller, who devoted himself to helping poor travellers. The name came to Britain in the 13th century in the Latin form, which was anglicized as **Julyan**, and in the North of England as **Jolyon**. Julian became popular in the 19th century, and today is quite a common name. Jolyon was used by John Galsworth in his *Forsyte Saga* novels, and this helped the form become better known. **Jules**, the French form of JULIUS, is also used as a short form of the name, as are **Jule** and occasionally **Julie**.

JULIANA *f.* (*jŏŏliān'e*)

This is the feminine form of JULIAN. St Juliana was an early Christian martyr, whose relics are said to have been taken to Brussels, and it has been suggested that the name first came to Britain in the 12th century from the Low Countries. A prioress in St Albans, whose name was **Julian** (the old form of the name) or Juliana, wrote a treatise on field sports in the 15th century, and in the same century Julian of Norwich wrote *Revelations of Divine Love*. The variant forms GILLIAN and **Jill** were among the commonest girl's names from the 12th to the 15th centuries. The name subsequently dropped out of popular use but was revived in the 18th century. Gillian is probably the most popular form today. It shares the short form **Julie** with **Julia**. (*see* LIANNE).

JULIANUS *see* JULIAN

JULIE *see* JULIA

JULIET *f.* (*jŏŏ'liet*)

This is a short form of the Italian **Giulietta**, a diminutive of JULIA. Its use nowadays is probably the result of the influence of Shakespeare's *Romeo and Juliet*. **Juliette** is a French form sometimes used in Britain.

JULIUS *m.* (*jŏŏ'lies*)

the name of the Roman clan to which Caius Julius Caesar belonged. The meaning of the name is not certain, since, although it can be translated as 'hairy', this might be in the Greek sense of 'downy bearded', and hence 'clean-shaven'. The name has never been used much in Britain, but there was a judge named Julius Caesar who was knighted in 1603, and his family continued the tradition of combining the two names. Today JULIAN, a derivative, is far more common.

JULYAN *see* JULIAN

JUNE *f.* (*jóon*)

This is simply the name of the month which, like April, has been used as a girl's name in the 20th century.

JUNO *see* UNA

JUSTIN *m.*, JUSTINE *f.* (*jus'tin, justēn'*)

from the Latin, meaning 'just'. These were uncommon names until twenty years ago, when they came back into fashion. **Justina** is the old feminine form, but the French **Justine** is now used, possibly made better known by Lawrence Durrell's novel of that title.

K

KAI *see* **KAY, CAIUS**

KAREL *see* **CAROL**

KAREN *f.* (*ka<u>re</u>n, kà<u>re</u>n*)

a Scandinavian form of KATHARINE. It was only introduced into this country in the 1930s, but has been very popular. Variants include **Karan** and **Karin**.

KARENZA *see* **KERENSA**

KARL *see* **CARL**

KASPAR *see* **JASPER**

KATHARINE, KATHERINE, CATHARINE, CATHERINE *f.* (*kath'rin*)

from Greek *katharos*, meaning 'pure'. The name came to England in the early 12th century when crusaders brought back the legend

of St Katharine of Alexandria. She was an
Egyptian princess who was tortured and put to
death in the early 4th century for her learned
defence of Christianity. The legend and the
name became very popular in Britain, and
today it is one of the commonest of all girl's
names. The most common short forms have
been **Kate**, **Kitty**, **Katie** and recently **Cathy**
and KAY. The Irish form **Kathleen** or
Cathleen is now used throughout Britain.
Caitlin is the older Irish form which has
recently become popular. There are a large
number of different spellings for the name, of
which **Kathryn** is one of the most frequent
(*see also* CATRIONA, KAREN).

KAY *m. and f.* (kā)

a pet form of names beginning with a K, such
as Katharine. It has been used as a first name
for the last hundred years, and can also be
spelt **Kai** and **Kaye** (*see also* CAIUS).

KEIRAN *see* KIERAN

KEITH *m.* (kēth)

This is a popular first name from Scotland
which has spread throughout Britain. It is
taken from the Scottish place name, which is

211

probably derived from the Gaelic for 'wood' or 'windy place'.

KELLY *f. and m.* (ke'lē)

a modern first name which has rapidly become very popular. It is the Irish surname, which means 'warlike', used as a first name. It is more usual as a girl's name than a boy's

KELVIN *m.* (kel'vin)

This name can be interpreted as from Old English, meaning 'ship-friend', but is more probably the name of the Scottish river used as a first name.

KEN, KENNY *see* KENNETH

KENELM *m.* (ken'elm)

from Old English, meaning 'brave helmet'. The 9th-century martyr, St Kenelm, King of Mercia, was venerated in the Midlands, where the Christian name flourished and is still in use.

KENNETH *m.* (ken'eth)

an anglicized derivative of the Gaelic **Coinneach**, meaning 'handsome', and equivalent to modern Welsh **Cenydd**. This is basically a Scottish name which became popular when Kenneth MacAlpine became first King of Scotland in the 9th century, uniting the Picts and the Scots. From Scotland it gradually spread over Britain. It is often shortened to **Ken** or **Kenny**.

KENT *m.* (*kent*)

the surname, taken from the English county, used as a first name. It first became popular in the United States.

KENTIGERN *see* MUNGO

KENTON *m.* (*kent'en*)

a common place name, meaning 'royal manor', used as a first name.

KERENSA, KERENZA *f.* (*keren'ze*)

a Cornish name meaning 'affection, love'. It is also found in the form **Karenza**.

KERRIDWEN *see* CERIDWEN

KERRY *m. and f. (kere)*

the Irish county used as a name. It was first
used in Australia as a male name, as in the
case of the businessman Kerry Packer, but is
now in general use, mainly for girls.

KESTER *see* **CHRISTOPHER**

KEVIN *m. (ke'vin)*

from the Irish, meaning 'handsome birth'. This
name was very popular in Ireland on account
of St Kevin, a 6th-century hermit, who later
became abbot of Glendalough. It is now widely
used throughout the English-speaking world.

KEZIA(H) *f. (kezē'e)*

the Hebrew word for the spice cassia, and the
name of one of the daughters of Job in the
Bible. In the last century it was a frequent
name for American slave girls. It then fell out
of fashion, but there has been a recent revival
of its use. The form **Keshia** also occurs, and
short forms of the name are **Kizzie** and **Kissie**.

KIERAN *m. (kee'ren)*

This is a form of the Irish name **Ciaran**, meaning 'dark-haired'. It was the name of 15 Irish

saints. In the last two or three decades it has become increasingly popular. It is sometimes spelt **Keiran** or **Kieron**.

KIM *m. and f.* (*kim*)

probably from Old English *cynebeald*, meaning 'royally bold', through the surname Kimball. Rudyard Kipling's hero in the novel *Kim* (1901) used a shortened form of his true name, Kimball O'Hara, showing the use of the surname as a Christian name. More recently the name has been almost exclusively used for girls.

KIMBERL(E)Y *f.* (*kim'belē*)

This is another possible source of the name KIM. Kimberley is a diamond-mining town in South Africa, and the association with jewels seems to have encouraged its use. Since it began to be used in the 1940s it has spread rapidly and is now one of the most popular girl's names. There was also a brief fashion for Kimberley as a boy's name at the turn of the century, no doubt commemorating events of the Boer War, but this soon died out.

KIRK *m.* (*kek*)

a Scandinavian name meaning 'church' brought to prominence as a first name by the actor Kirk Douglas.

KIRSTY, KIRSTEN *f.* (*ke'sti, ker'stn*)

These are both forms of the name CHRISTINE. Kirsty was originally a Scottish pet form, while Kirsten comes from Scandinavia.

KISSIE, KIZZIE *see* **KEZIA(H)**

KIT *see* **CHRISTOPHER**

KITTY *see* **KATHARINE**

KLAUS *see* **NICHOLAS**

KORDEL, KORDULA *see* **CORDELIA**

KURT *see* **CONRAD**

KYLE *m. and f.* (*kīl*)

This is a Scottish place and surname, meaning 'a strip of land'. It is more usual as a name for boys than girls.

KYLIE *f.* (*kī'le*)

This is an Australian name, taken from an Aborigine word meaning 'a curl'. It is best known in this country through the actress and singer Kylie Minogue.

L

LACHLAN *m.* (*laH'len*)

from Gaelic, meaning 'warlike'. Lochlann is
Gaelic for Norway. This is primarily a High-
land name, but there has recently been a
growth of interest in it in Australia.

LAETITIA *see* **LETTICE**

LAMBERT *m.* (*lam'bet*)

from the Old German, meaning 'land famous'.
The name was common in England from the
12th to the 15th centuries. It was brought over
by Flemish weavers from the Low Countries,
where the name was popular because of the
7th-century St Lambert, Bishop of Maastricht.
In Britain, it is best known for Lambert
Simnel, who tried to oust Henry VII from the
throne. It has been used occasionally since the
19th century.

LANA *see* **ALAN**

LANCELOT *m.* (*làn'selot*)

possibly a variant of the French Lance, from the Old German for 'land'. It can also be spelt **Launcelot**, and this form, along with **Lancelin**, was used in Britain from the 13th century, but only Lancelot survived. This was due to the popularity of Sir Lancelot in the stories of King Arthur. The name is more often found in its short form, **Lance**, today.

LARAINE *see* LORRAINE

LARRIE, LAURIE *see* LAURENCE

LAURA *f.* (*law're*)

Laura is derived, like LAWRENCE, from the Latin for 'laurel', a symbol, in the classical world, of victory and poetic genius. **Lauretta** is the diminutive form. Together with **Laurencia** and **Lora** these names were common from the 12th century. **Lauren, Lora** and **Lori** are popular variants of the name. Other diminutives which are sometimes used are **Laureen, Laurene,** and **Laurissa, Loretta** and **Lolly. Laurel,** the plant name, sometimes spelt **Lorel,** is also found.

LAURAINE *see* LORRAINE

LAURENCE, LAWRENCE m. (lor'ens)

from the Latin, meaning 'of Laurentium', a town which took its name from the laurel plant, symbol of victory. It became common in the 12th century. St Laurence, the 3rd-century Archdeacon of Rome, was a favourite medieval saint. It was popular in Ireland because of St Laurence O'Toole, a 12th-century Archbishop of Dublin, whose real name was **Lorcan** (Irish 'fierce'). **Larrie** or **Larry** is the usual abbreviation in England, while **Laurie** is used in Scotland. Such surnames as Laurie, Lowrie, Lawson and Larkin are derivatives.

LAURENCIA, LAUREEN, LAURENE, LAURISSA see LAURA

LAVINIA f. (levin'ie)

The meaning of this name is unknown, but in classical legend it was the name of Aeneas' wife, for whose hand he fought and defeated a rival suitor. The town Lavinium, originally called Latium, was renamed after her. The name was very popular for a while during the Renaissance, but then faded out, only returning to fashion in the 18th century. It is still used occasionally.

LEA *see* **LEE, LEO**

LEAH *f.* (lē'e)

a Hebrew word, probably meaning 'cow'. In the Bible Leah was the sister of Rachel, and first wife of Jacob. **Lia** the Italian form of the name, is sometimes used.

LEANNE *see* **LIANNE**

LEANORA *see* **LEONORA**

LEE, LEIGH, LEA *m. and f.* (lē)

from the various forms of the surname, meaning 'meadow'. The popularity of this name in the southern United States, from whence it has spread, probably owes something to the Confederate general Robert E. Lee (1807-70).

LEIGH ANN *see* **LIANNE**

LEILA *f.* (lēle)

a Persian name meaning 'dark-haired'. Byron started the fashion for it in the 19th century by using it in a poem with an oriental setting called *The Giaour*. The name appeared in the Persian romantic legend of **Leilah** and

Mejnoun, equivalent to the story of Cupid and Psyche of the Greeks. It is now fairly popular.

LEN, LENNIE, LENNY, LENNARD *see* LEONARD

LENA *see* HELEN

LENORE *see* LEONORA

LEO *m.*, LEONIE *f.* (*le̱'o*, *leōn'e*)

from the Latin meaning 'lion'. It was the name of six emperors of Constantinople and of thirteen popes. Léon and Lyon were fairly common medieval forms. The politician Leon Brittan shows the French form of the name, from which the feminine form Leonie comes. Other versions of the name used for girls include **Lea**, **Leola**, **Leona** and **Leontine** (*see* LIONEL).

LEOLIN, LEOLINE *see* LLEWELYN

LEON *see* LEO, LIONEL

LEONARD *m.* (*len'ed*)

from the Old German, meaning 'lion brave'. The 6th-century St **Leonhard** was a Frankish nobleman who was converted to Christianity.

He became a hermit, and devoted his life to helping prisoners, of whom he is the patron saint. His popularity made the name common in medieval England and France. The name was revived in the 19th century and is now fairly common. The usual shortened forms are **Len, Lennie** and **Lenny.** It is sometimes spelt **Lennard.**

LEONIE *see* LEO

LEONORA, LENORE, LEONORE *f.*
(*lēonaw're, lenaw', leo'naw*)

These names are European derivatives of ELEANOR, all of which have been used from time to time in this country. None of them appeared in Britain before the 19th century and their introduction was probably due to literary and musical influences. A short form which is fairly common is NORA.

LEOPOLD *m.* (*lē'epōld*)

from the Old German, meaning 'people bold'. This name came to Britain through Queen Victoria's uncle, King Leopold of Belgium, after whom she named her fourth son, the Duke of Albany. It has not been used much in the 20th century.

LEROY *m.* (*lē′roi*)

a surname meaning 'the King' which was probably given to royal servants, used as a first name. It has been particularly used in the United States.

LESLIE, LESLEY *m. and f.* (*lez′li*)

These were respectively the usual masculine and feminine spellings of the name, although they are used interchangeably. It is a Scottish surname used originally by the Lords of Leslie in Aberdeenshire. It was taken into general use as a Christian name in the late 19th century.

LESTER *m.* (*les′te*)

This is a surname of uncertain etymology but probably taken from the town of Leicester, which is sometimes used as a first name. Famous modern examples are Lester Pearson, the Canadian statesman, and Lester Piggott the English jockey.

LETTICE, L(A)ETITIA *f.* (*let′is, letish′e*)

from the Latin, meaning 'gladness'. Lettice was the usual form of this name from the 12th to the 17th centuries, during which time it was very popular. In the 18th century the Latin Laetitia superseded it, sometimes reduced to Letitia. None of these names is particularly common at present, though Lettice did return briefly in the late 19th and early 20th century. The short forms **Lettie** and **Letty** are sometimes used independently.

LEWIS, LOUIS m. (lŏŏ'is, lŏŏ'i)

from Old German Chlodowig, meaning 'famous warrior', which was latinized into **Ludovicus**, giving us **Ludovic**, and, in the French form, **Clovis**. Clovis was the name of the founder of the French monarchy. He became Louis, and this was the name of eighteen French Kings. The Normans brought the name to England where it became **Lewis** and sometimes **Lowis**. The use of the French Louis is comparatively recent; Robert Louis Stevenson is an early example, and this form is quite common in the lowlands of Scotland. In Wales, Lewis has been used to anglicize LLEWELYN. Short forms are **Lou** and **Louie**, or **Lew** and **Lewie**.

LEX *see* **ALEXANDER**

LIA *see* **LEAH**

LIAM see **WILLIAM**

LIANNE, LEANNE f. (lēan')

a pet form of the name JULIANA which has recently become popular as an idependent name. It can also be spelt **Liane** and occurs in such forms as **Leigh Anne**.

LIBBY see **ELIZABETH**

LIESEL see **ELIZABETH**

LILIAN, LILY f. (lil'i̲e̲n, lil'i)

Originally these names may have been pet forms of ELIZABETH. **Lillian** is found in Shakespeare's time but the name was probably associated with the Lily flower even then. In the 19th century Lily was definitely given as the name of the flower, which is a Christian symbol of purity. **Lil** is the usual abbreviation. Other forms of the name include **Lillah** and, in Scotland, **Lillias**.

LILITH f. (lil'ith)

from the Hebrew, meaning either 'serpent' or 'belonging to night'. In semitic mythology Lilith was an evil spirit who haunted the night and who had been Adam's rejected wife before Eve. The name has been used very rarely.

LILLAH, LILLIAN, LILLIAS *see* LILIAN

LINA *f.* (*lē'ne*)

a short form of names ending in '-lina', such as Angelina and Carolina, used as an independent name.

LIN(N)(E) *see* LINDA, LYNNE

LINDA, LINDY *see* BELINDA

LINDA *f.* (*lin'de*)

This was a common ending for girls' names in Old German, and comes from the word for a snake, an animal which was held in great reverence by primitive Germanic tribes. Its attributed qualities were wisdom and suppleness, and the names derived from it were therefore complimentary. In Spanish *linda* means pretty, and this may also have had some effect on the use of Linda as an English first name, which only dates from the 19th century. It is also used as a contraction of BELINDA. It is also spelt **Lynda**, and **Lindy**, **Lin** and LYN are pet forms.

LINDSEY *m. and f. (lin'zi)*

from the Scottish surname meaning 'pool island'. Together with its other forms **Lindsay**, **Linsey**, and **Linsay**, this name is used for both boys and girls. The form Lindsay tends to be the more usual one for boys. At the moment all forms of the name are used more frequently for girls than for boys.

LINDY *see* **LINDA**

LINETTE *see* **LYNETTE**

LINSAY, LINSEY *see* **LINDSEY**

LIONEL *m. (lī'onel)*

a French diminutive of Léon, meaning 'young lion'. It was the name of one of King Arthur's knights and was given by Edward III to his third son, later Duke of Clarence. The name was popular in the Middle Ages and survived in the North of England, whence it has come back into general, though infrequent use (*see* LEO).

LISA, LIZA *see* **ELIZABETH**

LISE, LISETTE *see* **ELIZABETH**

LIZ, LIZZY *see* ELIZABETH

LLEWELLYN, LLYWELYN *m.* (*lóòwel'in, hlewel'in*)

from Welsh. The meaning is doubtful but is possibly 'like a lion'. It is an old Welsh name which was anglicized into **Leolin(e)** as early as the 13th century. This form was used at least until the 17th century, when Lewis replaced it. Llewelyn, properly Llywelyn, is one of the commonest Christian names in Wales. **Lyn** is a short form.

LLOYD *m.* (*loid, hloid*)

a Welsh Christian name, meaning 'grey'. **Floyd** is a variant form which has arisen owing to the difficulty of pronouncing the Welsh 'Ll'. It is mainly found in North America. A famous example is Floyd Patterson, a former heavyweight boxing champion.

LO, LOLITA *see* DOLORES, LOLA

LOIS *f.* (*lō'is*)

In the New Testament, Lois was the grandmother of Timothy. As the rest of the family had Greek names, Lois is probably Greek also, but its meaning is not known. Like many obscure Biblical names, it was taken into use in the 17th century by Puritans. It fell out of use but was revived at the beginning of the 20th century.

LOLA *f.* (lō'le)

This was originally a diminutive of the Spanish DOLORES and of Carlotta. It has occasionally been used in North America and in Britain, where the name has been given to a famous breed of racing cars. The diminutive **Lolita** has become well-known in the 20th century through Vladimir Nabokov's novel of that name.

LORA, LORETTA *see* LAURA

LORAINE *see* LORRAINE

LORNA *f.*, LORNE *m.* (law'ne, lawn)

This name was created by R.D. Blackmore for the heroine of his novel *Lorna Doone*. He may have had in mind the Marquis of Lorne or the Old English word meaning 'lost', 'forsaken'. Since the publication of the book in 1869, the name has been quite popular. The actor **Lorne**

Green shows the masculine name that developed from it.

LORRAINE f. (lorān')

This is the French form of the Old German place name Lotharingen, meaning 'from Lothar's place'. Lothar was an Old German warrior name meaning 'famous army'. Lorraine is a first name in France, and has been borrowed with growing frequency in Britain and North America, sometimes in the forms **Loraine**, **Laraine** or **Lauraine**. **Lori** is a pet form.

LOTTIE, LOTTY see CHARLOTTE

LOU, LOIE see LEWIS, LOUSIA

LOUELLA see LUELLA

LOUIS see LEWIS

LOUISA, LOUISE f. (lóoēz'e, lóoēz')

Louise is the French, and Louisa the Latin, feminine form of Louis (see LEWIS). Though common much earlier in France, Louise did not come to Britain until the 17th century, when Louise de Keroual became Charles II's favourite. It was popular for about a century until Louisa superseded it. Today both are about equally common. Pet forms are **Lulu**, **Lou** and **Lonie**.

LOWIS *see* **LEWIS**

LUCAS *see* **LUKE**

LUCASTA, LUCETTE *see* **LUCY**

LUCE, LUCIA *see* **LUCY**

LUCILLE *f.*, **LUCIUS** *m.* (*lōōsēl'*, *lōō'sies*)

from the Latin word *lux*, meaning 'light' (*see* LUCY). **Lucilla** retains the Latin diminutive form, while **Lucille** is French. The male form Lucius and its variants, **Lucien** and **Lucian**, are much less common than the feminine names.

LUCINA *see* **LUCY**

LUCINDA *f.* (*loosin'de*)

Originally a poetic form of LUCY, this name is now given independently, and has recently become quite popular. The short form **Cindy** is sometimes used as a name in its own right.

LUCRETIA f. (lóokre̱')

This is a Roman family name derived from the Latin for 'profit' or 'riches'. Its use as a first name in Renaissance Europe was due to Lucretia, the wife of Collatinus, who was raped by Tarquin and committed suicide. This incident led to the expulsion of the Tarquins from Rome. Shakespeare's poem *The Rape of Lucrece* spread the use of the name in this form. It was most common in Britain between the 16th and the 18th centuries but has never quite died out.

LUCY f. (lóo'si)

Lucy is the usual English form of the Latin Lucia, from *lux*, meaning 'light'. In Roman times, the name often signified that the child had been born at dawn; the goddess **Lucina** was the patroness of childbirth, bringing the children into the light of day. St Lucy was a Sicilian martyr who was much beloved in the Middle Ages, and the name became well established after the Norman Conquest, with the alternative form **Luce**. The Latin **Lucia** was used from the 17th century but Lucy is the current form, which is very common in Britain. Other diminutives and derivatives are **Lucette**, LUCINDA, **Lucasta** and **Lulu**.

LUDOVICUS *see* LEWIS

LUELLA *f.* (*lŏoel'e*)

probably from the Old English meaning 'famous elf'. Another possible source is a combination of the names LOUISE and ELLA. Today the name is most popular in North America. **Louella** is an alternative spelling.

LUKE *m.* (*lŏok'*)

from Greek, latinized as **Lucas**, meaning 'a man of Lucania' in southern Italy. St Luke the Evangelist is the patron saint of doctors and also of painters, and the name was often given by a craftsman to his son. The name appeared in the 12th century as Lucas but a century later it was well established in the English form Luke. It has been a very popular name in recent years.

LULU *see* LOUISA, LUCY

LUNED *see* ELUNED

LUTHER _m._ (lŏŏ'the)

from the Old German, meaning 'famous
warrior'. The modern use of Luther as a
Christian name is entirely due to Martin
Luther, the great German religious leader of
the Reformation, and to the American civil
rights campaigner Martin Luther King,
named after him.

LYDIA _f._ (lĭd'ie)

from the Greek meaning 'a Lydian girl'. Lydia
was a district of Asia Minor where the people
were famous merchants, and were said to have
invented coinage. In the Acts of the Apostles,
Lydia was a widow of Philippi, who was converted by St Paul when he stayed at her house.
The name was not used in this country before
the 17th century.

LYN _see_ **LLEWELLYN, LYNNE**

LYNDA _see_ **LINDA**

LYNETTE _f._ (linet')

from the Welsh name ELUNED via its short
form Luned. The form Lynette was introduced
by the poet Tennyson in the story of _Gareth_

and Lynette in his *Idylls of the King*. It is also spelt **Linet**, **Linnet**, **Linette** and **Lynnette**, and LYNN is used as a short form.

LYN(N)(E) *f. (lin)*

a short form of such names as LINDA, LYNETTE and CAROLYN, popular as an independent name.

LYON *see* LEO

M

MABEL (*mā'bel*)

Mabel is a shortening of AMABEL, **Mabella** is the latinized form. Both were current from the 12th to the 15th century, but were rare thereafter. Mabel was revived in the 19th century and became very common. It has recently suffered another fall from favour. Such surnames as Mabbs, Mabbot and Mappin are derivations. The pet form often used is MAY. **Maybelle** and **Maybelline** are developments of the name.

MACSEN *see* MAXIMILIAN

MADEL(E)INE, MAGDALEN(E) *f.*
(*mad'elin, mag'delin, mag'delēn*)

Magdalene, the original form of the name, is Hebrew, and means 'woman of Magdala', a town on the Sea of Galilee which was the birthplace of St Mary Magdalene. From about the 12th century the name was used in

England in the French form Madeline, often abbreviated to **Maudlin** and **Madlin**. Magdalen, the Biblical form, was adopted after the Reformation. It was usually pronounced like **Maudlin**, but, because the meaning of this word developed into the sense of weak and sentimental, this form was replaced by the current Madeline or one of a number of other spellings of the name. It shares the short form **Madge** with Margaret. **Maddie** or **Maddy** is also used. Another short form is **Magda**, which has also been given as an independent name.

MADGE *see* **MADELINE, MARGARET**

MADLIN, MAUDLIN *see* **MADELINE**

MADOC, MADOG *m.* (*mad'ek, mad'eq*)

from the Welsh meaning 'fortunate'. This name is most common in Wales. There is some evidence of its use in the West of England in the 11th century, lasting until the 15th century. It is very rarely used outside Wales today.

MAELMOR *see* **MILES**

MAERWINE *see* **MERVYN**

MAEVE f. (*mav*)

the usual form of the Irish name **Meadhbh**, meaning 'joy'. It was the name of a famous queen in Irish legend. A diminutive is **Meaveen**, and the name is occasionally spelt **Meave**.

MAGDA *see* **MADELINE**

MAGGIE *see* **MARGARET**

MAGNUS m. (*mag'nes*)

This is the Latin adjective meaning 'great'. The spread of this name was due to the Emperor Charlemagne, Carolus Magnus. Some of his admirers took Magnus for a personal name, and among those who christened their sons after him was St Olaf of Norway. The name spread from Scandinavia to Shetland and Ireland. From Shetland the name became well established in Scotland. In Ireland it became **Manus**, hence the common Irish surname McManus.

MAHALIA f. (*mehā'lēe*)

a form of the Hebrew **Mahala** meaning 'tenderness'. No longer a very usual name, it is best known from the singer Mahalia Jackson.

MAI, MAIA *see* **MAY**

MAIRE *see* **MARY**

MAIRIN *see* **MAUREEN**

MAISIE *see* **MARGARET**

MALCOLM *m.* (*mal'kem*)

from the Gaelic, meaning 'follower of St
Columba'. This is a very popular Scottish
name, and four kings of Scotland bore it. It
was used very occasionally in medieval
England, but it is only in this century that it
has become common. Short forms are **Mal** and
Calum (*see* COLUM).

MALVINA *f.* (*malvē'ne*)

a name invented by the Scottish poet James
Macpherson (1736-96). He may have meant it
to be understood to be from the Gaelic meaning
'smooth brow'. The form **Melvina** is also found.

MAMIE *see* **MARY**

MANDY *see* **AMANDA**

MANNY, MANUEL *see* **EMANUEL**

MANUS *see* **MAGNUS**

MAOLMUIRE *see* **MILES**

MAPPIN *see* **MABEL**

MARC, MARCEL *see* **MARCUS**

MARCIA *f.* (màs'ie, mà'she)

the feminine form of the Latin Marcius, a
Roman clan name. It probably came originally
from the name of the god Mars. St Marcia
was an early Christian martyr. The name's
popularity in Britain seems to have grown in
recent years, possibly developing as a feminine
version of MARCUS. The commonest variant
spelling is Marsha, with **Marcy** used as a short
form. **Marcella**, **Marcelle**, **Marcelline** and
Marcine are all developments of the name.

MARCIUS *see* **MARCIA**

MARCUS, MARK *m.* (mà'kes, màk)

from the name of Mars, the Roman god of war,
and a well-known Roman family name and
personal name. Although the name occurs
from the Middle Ages in Britain, it has become
common since the 1950s. Latin form Marcus is

the less common of the two. The modern use
of the name is due to the Evangelist St Mark.
In the Middle Ages Venetian merchants captured St Mark's relics from Alexandria and
took them back to Venice where they built
the magnificient basilica in his honour. The
Venetians were also the bankers of Europe at
this time and their coinage bore the symbol of
St Mark, a winged lion, and was therefore
called a 'mark'. Samuel L. Clements (1835-
1910) made the name familiar with his pen
name 'Mark Twain' (from a call by Mississippi
boatmen indicating water depth). The French
forms **Marc** and **Marcel**, the latter derived
from the Latin diminutive **Marcellus**, are also
used in Britain today.

MARCY *see* **MACIA**

MAREDUDD *see* **MEREDITH**

MARGARET *f.* (*ma'gerit*)

from the Latin *margarita*, derived from the
Greek word meaning 'a pearl', although the
ultimate origin is thought to be Persian, for
'child of light'. Apparently the Persians
believed that pearls were formed when oysters
rose from their beds at night to look at the

moon, and trapped a drop of dew in their shells, which was transformed into a pearl by the moonbeams. The name first spread into Scotland in the 11th century on account of St Margaret, wife of Malcolm III. She was of Hungarian extraction, the name having penetrated into Eastern Europe through the influence of St Margaret of Antioch, a 3rd-century martyr. The name became very common in medieval England and, after a decline, regained its enormous popularity in the 19th century. This has persisted to the present day. The most common pet forms are **Madge**, **Meg** and **Peg**(**gy**). **Maisie** and **Maggie** are particularly Scottish variants, and **Megan** the Welsh. Other diminutives sometimes used are the German and Swedish GRETA, French **Margot** and **Marguerite**, and Italian **Rita**, from **Margarita**. Other forms include **Marghanita**, **Margaretta** and **Margoletta** (see also DAISY, MARGERY, MAY).

MARGERY, MARJORIE f. (mà'jeri)

Margerie was originally a pet form of the French Marguerite, but it became established as a proper name in England as early as the 12th century. Marjorie is the spelling in Scotland, where the name was popular from the late 13th century, after Robert Bruce gave the name to his daughter. She later founded the Stuart dynasty by marrying Walter the High Steward. **Marge** and **Margie** are pet forms.

MARGHANITA *see* MARGARET

MARGOT, MARGOLETTA *see* MARGARET

MARGUERITE *see* MARGARET, MARGERY

MARIAM *see* MIRIAM

MARIA, MIRIAM, MARIE *see* MARY

MARIAN, MARION *f. (mar'ien)*

This name was originally a diminutive of the French Marie (*see* MARY), which was early established as an independent name, and was common on both sides of the English Channel in medieval times. Maid Marian is well-known as Robin Hood's sweetheart. Marian was a later form which was extended to **Marianne**, giving rise to the double name **Mary Anne** in the 18th century. **Marianna** is a Spanish equivalent which is sometimes given in England. The word 'marionette' is a derivative of the name. **Marion** is occasionally found as a masculine name, as in the case of Marion Morrison, real name of actor John Wayne (1907-79).

MARIE, MARIEL, MARIETTA *see* MARY

MARIGOLD *f.* (mar'igōld)

This name, borrowed from the flower, was adopted with others in the late 19th century, but has never become common.

MARILYN *f.* (mar'elin)

This is a diminutive of MARY now used independently. Its popularity was heightened by the film actress Marilyn Monroe (1926-62).

MARINA *f.* (merē'ne)

from the Latin *marinus*, meaning 'of the sea'. The name has been used occasionally from at least the 14th century, probably on account of St Marina of Alexandria, a martyr of the Greek church. The name became more popular in Britain in 1934, when Prince George married

Princess Marina of Greece, who later became Duchess of Kent.

MARIO *see* **MARIUS**

MARION *see* **MARIAN**

MARIOT *see* **MARY**

MARISA *see* **MARY**

MARIUS *m.* (*màr'ies*)

from a Roman family name, which was first adopted for use during the Renaissance. It has never been common in this country, although **Mario** is very popular in Italy. The name is probably a derivative of Mars, the Roman god of war and thunder.

MARJORIE *see* **MARGERY**

MARK *see* **MARCUS**

MARLENE *f.* (*mà'lēn, màlā'ne*)

a German shortening of Mary Magdalene (see MADELEINE). It was introduced to English speakers by the song *Lili Marlene* and by the actress Marlene Dietrich (b.1901). **Marlena** is also used.

MARLON m. (mà'lon)

a name of unknown origin, brought into use through the fame of the actor Marlon Brando (b.1924).

MARMADUKE m. (mà'medūk)

from the Irish, meaning 'servant of MADOC'. The influence of the Normans on the English language after the Conquest, gave rise to the medieval spelling **Marmaduc**. The name is mainly confined to Yorkshire, which was probably an outpost of Celtic civilization in the North of England. **Duke** is sometimes used as an abbreviation in the North, but in North America its use is usually derived purely from the title, and **Earl**, **Count** and **King** are also found.

MARSHA see MARCIA

MARTHA f. (mà'the)

from the Aramaic, meaning 'lady'. In the new Testament Martha was the sister of Lazarus and Mary Magdalene. She is described as being a good and careful housewife. The name was common in France in the Middle Ages, where there was a legend that Martha had travelled to France after the Crucifixion. It was not adopted in Britain until after the Reformation. The name became fairly common, possibly aided to some extent by Flotow's popular opera *Martha* (1847). Variants include **Marta**, **Martita** and **Martella**. **Marty** is the commonest pet form.

MARTIN *m.*, MARTINA *f.* (*mà'tin, màtē'ne*)

from the Latin Martinus, a diminutive of Martius, meaning 'of Mars'. Mars was the Roman god of thunder and war. According to popular legend, St Martin was a 4th-century soldier who cut his cloak in two to give half to a beggar one winter's night. He later became Bishop of Tours in France. He also gave his name to two birds, the martin and the martlet. This was the name of five popes and also of Martin Luther, the great Protestant reformer, so it has been very popular in both churches. It has been used more or less without a break since the 12th century and today is more popular than ever. It is sometimes spelt **Martyn** with

Marty as a short form. **Martina** and **Martita**, the latter shared with MARTHA, are rare forms.

MARTINA, MARTITA *see* MARTIN, MARTHA

MARTINUS, MARTIUS *see* MARTIN

MARTY *see* MARTHA, MARTIN

MARTYN *see* MARTIN

MARVIN *m.* (mà'vin)

An old Welsh name, of unknown meaning.

MARY *f.* (mer'i)

from the Hebrew, probably meaning 'wished-for child'. The earliest form of the name was MIRIAM and later translations of the Bible changed this to Mariam and Maria, and finally Mary. The name was held to be too sacred for general use until about the 12th century. The French form **Marie**, and the diminutives MARION and **Mariot**, were all common. The name was very popular in England until the time of Mary I, 'Bloody Mary', and then Mary Queen of Scots, after which it became unfashionable in some cirles. The name did not entirely recover until the mid-17th century. The Scots retained the French **Marie** and the Gaelic **Mhairi**, **Maire** was the Irish form, and **Mair** the Welsh. The latinized **Maria** was adopted in the 18th century, giving a pet form of **Ria**. **Marise** and **Marisa** are continental forms of the name. **Mariel**, **Marietta** and **Manon** are also found. Pet forms of Mary are **Molly**, **Polly**, **Minnie**, **Mimi**, **Mamie** and MAY (*see also* MARIAN, MARILYN, MAUREEN, MIRIAM, MOIRA).

MARYANN(E) *see* **MARIAN**

MATHEU *see* **MATTHEW**

MATILDA *f.* (me̱til'de)

from the Old German, meaning 'mighty battlemaid'. This name was particularly popular in medieval Court circles, and was introduced by William the Conqueror's wife who bore the name. Later their granddaughter, sometimes known as MAUD, fought to oust her cousin Stephen from the throne. The name fell into disuse but returned to favour in the 18th century. **Matty** and **Tilly** are pet forms. Matilda is best known today in the popular Australian song *Waltzing Matilda*.

MATTHEW, MATTHIAS m. (math'ū, methī'es)

from the Hebrew, meaning 'gift of God', and the name of one of the Evangelists. In England the name first appears in Domesday Book, in the Latin form **Matthaeus** and the French **Matheu**, from which the usual English form Matthew is derived. The name was particularly popular from the 12th to the 14th centuries. After the Reformation Matthias was adopted, the name of the apostle chosen to succeed Judas Iscariot. Today the English form is fairly common, and the usual short form is **Matt**.

MAUD(E) f. (mawd)

from the Old French form of the name MATILDA. This name was popular in Britain after the Norman Conquest, but fell out of use about the 15th century. It was revived in the 19th century by Tennyson's well-known poem *Maud* (1855). **Maudie** is sometimes used as a pet form.

MAURA *see* **MOIRA**

MAUREEN f. (maw'rēn)

from the Irish **Mairin**, a diminutive of Maire (*see* MARY). The fashion for Maureen has probably come to England from North America. Another possible derivation is the Old French word meaning 'a Moor', which was the feminine form of MAURICE. The variant forms in Britain are **Moreen** and MOIRA.

MAURICE, MORRIS m. (mor'is)

from the Latin Mauritius, meaning 'a Moor'. The spread of the name was due to St Maurice, a 3rd-century martyr in Switzerland, after whom the town of St Moritz was named. The Normans brought the name to England as Meurisse, which was soon anglicized to Morris. A 'morris dance' is really a 'moorish dance'. The more modern French Maurice has now to a large extent replaced the English form, although it is pronounced the same way. In Ireland it has been used to translate the native **Moriarty**. There is a very old Welsh equivalent, **Meurig**, which occurs in the 5th century. Short forms are **Morrie** and **Maurie**.

MAVIS f. (mā'vis)

This is derived from the old word for a song thrush. It was first used by Marie Corelli in her novel *The Sorrows of Satan* (1895), for a character called Mavis Clare. Since then it has become fairly common in this country.

MAX *see* **MAXIMILIAN, MAXWELL**

MAXIMILIAN *m.* (*maximil'ien*)

Maximus in Latin means 'greatest'. Two 3rd-century saints bore the name Maximilian derived from it, but despite this, it is popularly thought to have been invented by the German Emperor Frederick III, combining the last names of Quintus Fabius Maximus, and Scipio Aemilianus, two great Roman generals. His son, later Emperor Maximilian I, was a reckless huntsman and fighter, and his name became very popular throughout Austria and German-speaking peoples. The name has occasionally been used in England, mainly by people of German extraction like Sir Max Beerbohm (1872-1956), author and caricaturist. **Max** and **Maxy** are the usual abbreviations. **Macsen** is the Welsh form of Maximus and **Maxime** the French.

MAXINE *f.* (*max'ēn*)

This is a feminine form of the name **Max**, and has come into use this century (*see* MAXIMILIAN).

MAXWELL *m.* (*maks'wel*)

from Old English, probably meaning 'great' and 'spring'. Though mainly a surname, it has been given as a first name in the last hundred years. **Max** is the short form.

MAY *f.* (*mā*)

This was originally a pet form of MARGARET or MARY but it has more recently been associated with the month (*see* JUNE, APRIL), and it is now a separate name. Variants are **Mae**, as in the actress Mae West (1892-1980), **Mai**, **Maia** and **Maya**.

MEAVE *see* MAEVE

MEG, MEGAN *see* MARGARET

MELANIE, MELLONEY *f.* (*mel'eni*)

from the Greek meaning 'black' or 'dark-skinned'. **Melania** is an ancient name known to both the Greeks and the Romans. The name came to England from France in the mid-17th century in the French form **Melanie**, which became Melloney and Melanie in Britain.

MELISENDA, MELISANDE, MELISENT
see MILLICENT

MELISSA *f.* (m<u>e</u>lis'<u>e</u>)

from the Greek meaning 'a bee'. This is the
name of a nymph, and also of the legendary
woman, murdered by her husband Periander,
ruler of Corinth, who wandered naked in the
underworld, because her funeral clothes had
not been ceremonially burned. It was used
occasionally in the 18th century, and has been
popular in recent years.

MELLONEY *see* MELANIE

MELODY *f.* (mel'od<u>e</u>)

The word, which has been used as a first name
in recent years.

MELVINA *see* MALVINA

MELVIN, MELVYN *m.* (melvin)

probably from the Irish, meaning 'polished
chief', a description of the knight's sword. It
has also been traced from Old English Mael-
wine, meaning 'sword friend' or 'speech friend'.
A well-known modern bearer of the name is

the television personality Melvyn Bragg. **Mel** is the short form.

MERCEDES *see* DOLORES

MERCY *f* (me͟'ce)

the virtue used as a first name. The pet form is **Merry**, which is also used as an independent name.

MEREDITH *m. and f.* (mer'edith)

from the Welsh **Maredudd**, meaning 'great chief', and widespread as a surname. It is sometimes spelt **Meridith**, and shares **Merry** with MERCY as a short form. It is rarely used for men outside Wales.

MERIEL *see* MURIEL

MERLE *f.* (mēl)

This is the French for 'blackbird' originally derived from Latin. It was adopted as a first name in the 19th century. It is well known as the name of the American film actress Merle Oberon (1911-79), and there is a Madame Merle in Henry James' novel *Portrait of a Lady* (1881). The name is rather rare today.

MERLIN *m.* (*me'lin*)

from the Welsh **Myrddin**, possibly meaning 'sea hill'. It was the name of a legendary poet and prophet of the 6th century, and of the magician in Arthurian legends. It is not often found.

MERRY *see* **MERCY, MEREDITH**

MERVYN *m.* (*me'vin*)

There are two possible etymologies for this very old name. There was an Anglo-Saxon name **Maerwine**, meaning 'famous friend'. Better known is Myrddin, Welsh 'sea hill', which is the true form of MERLIN, King Arthur's legendary magician. It is also spelt **Mervin**.

MERYL *see* **MURIEL**

MEURIG *see* **MAURICE**

MEURISSE *see* **MAURICE**

MHAIRI *see* **MARY**

MIA *f.* (*me'e*)

the Italian and Spanish word for 'my'. It is
particularly associated with the actress Mia
Farrow (b.1945).

MICHAEL *m.*, **MICHELLE** *f.* (*mīk'el,*
mēshel')

from the Hebrew meaning 'who is like the
Lord?' In the Bible Michael was one of the
seven archangels, and their leader in battle,
and therefore patron of soldiers. The name was
common from the 12th century but the spelling
and pronunciation varied considerably,
Machel, **Mihiel** and **Mighel** being the most
common. The variant form **Micah**, the name
of a minor prophet in the Old Testament, was
used in the 17th century among Puritans.
Michael is now common throughout Britain
and has pet forms **Mike**, **Mick**, **Micky**. Sometimes shortened to MILES. The surname **Mitchell**, derived from Michael, is also used as a
boy's name, with the short form **Mitch**. **Mich-
èle** is the French feminine form of the name,
which is anglicized to Michelle, and can be
shortened to SHELLEY. **Michaela** is another
feminine form of the name.

MILDRED *f.* (*mil'drid*)

The 7th-century King Merowald of the Old
English Kingdom of Mercia had three daughters: Milburga, 'gentle defence', Mildgyth,
'gentle gift', and Mildthryth, 'gentle strength'.
It was from the last of these that Mildred was
derived and the popularity of the three sisters,
all of whom were canonized, led to the name
becoming common in the Middle Ages. It was
revived in the 19th century.

MILES *m.* (*mīls*)

probably from one of the compounds of the Old
German root *mil*, meaning 'beloved'. Another
possible derivation is the Latin for 'soldier'.
The Normans brought to Britain the forms
Miles, **Milo** and **Milon**. Miles was quite a
popular name in the Middle Ages and it survived as a surname until its revival as a
Christian name in the 19th century. This
revival may have been partly due to the use
of the name in Ireland to transliterate the Irish
Maolmuire ('servant of Mary') and Maelmor
('majestic chief'). The name is sometimes used
as a reduction of Michael. A variant spelling
is **Myles**.

MILLICENT, MELICENT *f.* (*mil'is__ent,*
mel'is__ent)

from the Old German meaning 'strong worker'.
This name was common in France about a
thousand years ago, when it had the form
Melisenda, now also **Melisande**. The French
brought it to England in the late 12th century
in the form **Melisent**, and it survived with
minor changes of spelling well into the 17th
century. In the 19th and 20th centuries it
has been revived, ande Millicent is the most
common form, with **Milly** as a common
abbreviation.

MILLY *see* **AMELIA, CAMILLA, EMILY,
MILLICENT**

MILO, MILON *see* **MILES**

MILTON *m.* (*mil'ten*)

from the Old English surname meaning 'mill-
enclosure'. Its use as a first name comes from
the fame of the poet John Milton (1608-74). It
has been particularly popular in America.

MIMI *see* **MARY**

MINN *see* **MIRIAM**

MINNA, MINNIE *see* **MARY, MIRIAM, WILLIAM**

MINTA, MINTY *see* **ARAMINTA**

MIRA *see* **MYRA**

MIRABEL, MIRABELLE *f.* (*mir'abel*)

from the Latin, meaning 'wonderful'. The Latin form **Mirabella** was used in the past century, but it was later anglicized as Mirabel or Mirabelle.

MIRANDA *f.* (*miran'de*)

from the Latin, meaning 'to be admired'. This name was first used by Shakespeare for the heroine of *The Tempest* (1612), a young girl blessed with many admirable qualities. Like other unusual Shakespearian names it has been used quite frequently in the 20th century.

MIRIAM *f.* (*mir'iem*)

from the Hebrew, probably meaning 'wished-for child'. This is the oldest known form of MARY, and in the book of Exodus in the Old Testament, it was the name of the sister of Moses and Aaron. It first became common in

Britain in the 17th century. **Mariam** is a variant form which has recently gained popularity. Short forms which are sometimes found in connection with this name are **Minn**, **Minnie** and **Mitzi**.

MITCH, MITCHELL *see* MICHAEL

MITZI *see* MIRIAM

MOIRA, MOYRA *f.* (*moi're*)

an English rendering of the Irish Maire and Moire, Irish forms of MARY. The name has spread to Britain and America where it has flourished. **Maura** and MAUREEN have the same origin, but have developed quite independently as separate names, though Moira is very occasionally used as a short form of Maureen.

MOLLY *see* MARY

MONA *f.* (*mō'ne*)

This name is derived from a diminutive of the Irish *maudh*, meaning 'noble'. It came into use in the late 19th century along with other Irish names which spread throughout Britain at that time, during a general revival of interest in Celtic culture.

MONICA f. (mon'ik̲e̲)

The etymology of this name is uncertain, but it could be connected with Greek *monos* meaning 'alone' or Latin *moneo*, meaning 'to advise'. St Monica was the mother of St Augustine and was a paragon of motherly and wifely virtues. The name has become particularly popular in the 20th century. **Mona** is sometimes used as a short form, and there is a French form, **Monique**.

MONTAGU(E) m. (mon'teg̲ū̲)

The founder of this ancient and noble family was Drogo de Montacute, a companion of William the Conqueror, who was granted estates in Somerset. He took his name from Mont Aigu, a 'pointed hill' in Normandy. The use of Montagu(e) as a Christian name dates from the 19th century, when many aristocratic surnames were adopted by the general public, e.g. CECIL, HOWARD, DUDLEY, MORTIMER, PERCY. It shares **Monty** as a short form with Montgomery.

MONTGOMERY m. (*montgom'eri*)

from the Old French, meaning 'mountain of the rich one'. Though mainly a surname, it has occasionally been used as a first name in the last hundred years.

MORAG f. (*mo'rag*)

from the Gaelic, a diminutive of *mor(a)* meaning 'great'. Another possibility is that the name is a variant of Mary. In Gaelic it was formerly used as an equivalent of SARAH.

MORAY *see* **MURRAY**

MORCANT *see* **MORGAN**

MOREEN *see* **MAUREEN**

MORGAN m. and f. (*maw'gen*)

In its earliest form, **Morcant**, this name meant 'seabright' (*see* MURIEL), but it later absorbed another name, **Morien**, meaning 'seaborn'. In legend, King Arthur's wicked half-sister was called Morgan le Fay. Its earliest celebrated male bearer was the first recorded British heretic, who was known as Pelagius, a Greek rendering of the name.

MORIARTY *see* **MAURICE**

MORIEN *see* **MORGAN**

MORITZ *see* **MAURICE**

MORNA, MYRNA *f.* (*maw'ne̯, me̯'ne̯*)

Both these names come from the Irish name **Muirne**, which means 'beloved' or 'gentle'. Both have become common in other parts of Britain.

MORRIE, MAURIE *see* **MAURICE**

MORRIS *see* **MAURICE**

MORRISON *m.* (*mor'ison*)

from the Scottish clan name. Like many other surnames, it is now used occasionally as a first name, mainly among Scots.

MORTIMER *m.* (*maw'time̯*)

an aristocratic surname generally adopted as a first name in the 19th century. The surname was derived from a French place name, meaning 'dead sea'. The Mortimer family connect it with the Dead Sea in Palestine, where their ancestors fought in crusading times. The pet form **Morty** was also used independently in Ireland as a transliteration of the Irish name **Murtagh** ('sea man'). This was then lengthened to Mortimer, and in this way the name became established. The short form **Mort** is also used.

MORVEN m. and f. (maw'ven)

from the Irish meaning 'tall blonde one'. It is a predominantly Irish name.

MORWENNA f. (maw'wene)

from Welsh probably meaning 'maiden'. There was a saint of this name about whom little is known, and the name is confined to Wales and the West Country.

MOSES m. (mō'ziz)

The meaning of this name is uncertain and it is possibly Egyptian rather than Hebrew. It became common among Jews after their return from captivity in Babylon. In Britain it first appears in Domesday Book as **Moyses**, which became **Moyse** or **Moss** in general use. The present form, Moses, which was not used until the Reformation, is the form used in the Authorized Version of the Bible.

MOYRA *see* **MOIRA**

MUIR *m.* (*mūer'*)

This is a Scottish surname meaning 'moor', and sometimes spelt Mure. It is occasionally used as a first name among Scots. A famous example is Muir Mathieson, the conductor.

MUIRGHAEL *see* **MURIEL**

MUIRNE *see* **MORNA**

MUNGO *m.* (*mung'gō*)

This name was originally a term of affection given to St **Kentigern** by his followers, and, in Gaelic, it means 'beloved'. He was a 6th-century bishop of Glasgow and is generally known as St Mungo. The name is confined to Scotland and the most famous bearer was Mungo Park, the 18th-century explorer of the River Niger.

MURDO, MURDOCH m. (me͟'dō, me͟'doH)

This popular Scottish name is derived from the Gaelic meaning 'seaman', and is equivalent to the Irish Murtagh (*see* MORTIMER).

MURIEL, MERIEL f. (mūr'iel, mer'iel)

from the Irish **Muirghael**, meaning 'seabright'. The name came to England at the time of the Norman Conquest, through the many Celts who were settled in Brittany and Normandy. Both forms were in common use until the mid-14th century. Muriel was revived in the 19th century and Meriel has recently come back into use also. Muriel Spark (b.1918) is a well-known novelist. Other forms such as **Meryl** and **Merrill** have appeared in this century.

MURRAY m. (mur'i)

from the Gaelic, meaning 'sea'. The Scottish clan of Murray, or Moray, probably took its name from the Moray Firth in the northeast of Scotland. James Stuart, Earl of Moray, was half-brother of Mary Queen of Scots, and he acted as Regent when she was imprisoned in Loch Leven Castle. His fame gave rise to the use of **Moray** as a first name in Scotland, but today the form Murray is more common, with **Murry** in Ireland.

MURTAGH *see* MORTIMER

MYFANWY *f.* (*mifan'wi*)

a well-known Welsh name meaning 'my rare one'. The commonest short forms in Wales are **Fanny** and **Myfi**.

MYLES *see* MILES

MYRA *f.* (*mī're*)

This name appears to have been invented in the 16th century by Fulke Greville, Lord Brooke, for the object of his love poems, and until the 19th century it was used exclusively by poets and novelists. The most celebrated bearer of the name was Dame Myra Hess, the pianist. The variant form **Mira** is also found, but usually as a short form of MIRABEL or MIRANDA.

MYRDDIN *see* MERLIN, MERVYN

MYRNA *see* MORNA

MYRTILL(A) *see* MYRTLE

MYRON m. (mi'r_en_)

the Greek word for fragrant. It was the name of a famous sculptor in the 5th century BC.

MYRTLE f. (m_e_'tl)

one of the flower names, in this case a shrub, which, since the 19th century, has been used as a girl's name. The name is Greek, and in Ancient Greece the Myrtle was a symbol of victory. The variant form, **Myrtilla**, is also occasionally found.

N

NAB *see* **ABEL**

NADINE *f.* (*na′dēn*)

This is a French name which is derived from the Russian word for 'hope'. It is occasionally found in Britain, but only since the 20th century. The variant forms **Nada** and **Nadia** are also current.

NAN, NANNY *see* **ANN**

NANCY *f.* (*nan′si*)

This was originally a pet form of ANN, but has long been established as a name in its own right. **Nanette** and **Nana** are French forms.

NAOMI *f.* (*nā′ōmi*)

from the Hebrew, meaning 'pleasant'. In the Old Testament Naomi was the mother-in-law of Ruth, whose two sons died in Moab. The name was adopted with many other Old Testament names by the Puritans in the 17th century. It has recently increased in popularity.

NAT *see* NATHAN, NATHANIEL

NATALIE, NATALIA *f.* (*nat'eli, natàl'ie*)

from the Latin *natale domini*, meaning 'the birthday of the Lord'. Natalia and its diminutive, **Natasha**, are popular names in Russia. The French form **Natalie** is quite common on the Continent, but is also found occasionally in Britain. Natalie Wood (1938-81) was a well-known film actress. The short form **Netty** is sometimes used.

NATASHA *see* NATALIE

NATHAN *m.* (*nā'then*)

from the Hebrew meaning 'gift'. It is best known for the prophet in the Old Testament who condemned King David for putting Uriah in the front line of battle, so that he might be killed, and David could marry his widow, Bathsheba. It has recently become popular. The name shares the short form, **Nat**, with Nathaniel.

NATHANIEL *m.* (*nethan'iel*)

from the Hebrew meaning 'gift of God'. It was
the Christian name of the apostle who was
better known as Bartholomew. The name was
rare in Britain until after Shakespeare's use
of it in *Love's Labour Lost* (1594). This made
the name better known, but it is more common
in North America today than in Britain.
Nathaniel Hawthorne was a famous American
writer of the 19th century. Nat, the short form,
is shared with Nathan.

NEAL, NEIL *see* NIGEL

NED(DY) *see* EDWARD

NEL, NEEL, NELE *see* NIGEL

NELL(Y) *f.* (*nel, nel'i*)

the pet form of ELLEN, HELEN and ELEANOR. It
was already in use in Britain in the Middle
Ages, and a famous holder of the name was
Nell (Eleanor) Gwyn, mistress of Charles II.
The name is still fairly popular in Britain.

NELSON *m.* (*nel'sn*)

a surname meaning 'Neil's son' (*see* NIGEL). It
is used as a first name after Horatio Nelson
(1758-1805).

NERYS f. (ne'ris)

an unusual Welsh name, meaning 'lady', which has become widely known through the actress Nerys Hughes.

NESSA, NESSIE see AGNES

NEST, NESTA see AGNES

NET, NETTIE see ANTONY

NETTA, NETTIE see JANET

NETTY see NATALIE

NEVILLE m. (nev'el)

from the French surname Neuville, meaning 'new town'. It was introduced into England at the time of the Norman Conquest, when the Neville family, who came over with William the Conqueror, was very powerful. Their influence continued, but the name was not adopted as a first name until the 17th century. Famous holders of the name were Neville Chamberlain (1869-1940), Prime Minister of Britain at the outbreak of the Second World War, and **Nevil** Shute (1899-1960), the novelist. The latter shows a variant spelling.

NIALL *see* **NIGEL**

NICHOLAS *m.* (nik'ōles)

from the Greek, meaning 'victory of the people'. The name was very popular in the Middle Ages as a result of the influence of St Nicholas, who was the patron of children and sailors. The usual forms then were **Nicol**, and in Latin **Nicholaus**. The use of **Claus** in 'Santa Claus' is taken from the modern corruption of the German form **Klaus**. The name faded out at the time of the Reformation, but it is now one of the most popular first names in Britain. **Nick** and **Nicky** are the pet forms.

NICOLA, NICOLETTE *f.* (nik'ōle, nikōlet')

These are respectively the Italian and French feminine forms of NICHOLAS. Nicola was used as early as the reign of King John, when Nicola de Camville resisted the French attack on Lincoln. In modern times **Nicole** and **Nicolette** have become quite common in Britain. The names are also spelt **Nichola** and **Nichole**. **Nickie**, **Nikki** and **Nicci** are short forms shared with NICHOLAS. (*see* COLETTE).

NIGEL, NIALL, NEAL, NEIL *m.* (*nī'jel, nēl'*)

The origin of this name has been separately traced back to the Irish word *naidh*, meaning 'champion', and the Icelandic hero's name Njal. The Normans first brought the name to England as **Nel, Neel, Nele**. This was latinized as **Nigellus**, which was later thought to be a diminutive from *niger* meaning 'black', and the forms **Nigell, Nygell**, and eventually Nigel, became popular names in the Middle Ages. Various forms of Niall continued in use. Neil is common mostly in Scotland, while Niall is common in Ireland, and Neal in England.

NINA *f.* (*nē'ne*)

a pet form of various Russian names ending '-nina', which is now established in this country as a name in its own right.

NINIAN *m.* (*nin'ien*)

the name of a 5th-century saint who converted the Picts in the south of Scotland to Christianity. It is now found mostly in Scotland and, occasionally, in the north of England.

NITA *see* **JOANNA**

NOEL *m. and f.* (nō′el)

This is an old French name derived from *dies natalis*, meaning 'birthday'. The name refers to Christmas Day, and was often given to children born on that day. **Nowell** is an English spelling which is also used and **Noelle** is an alternative feminine form.

NORA(H) *f.* (naw′re)

an Irish abbreviation of HONORA, now used as a separate name. It is also found as a short form for ELEANOR and LEONORA. In Ireland the pet form **Noreen** is used.

NORMA *f.* (naw′me)

possibly from the Latin, meaning 'rule' or 'precept'. The name was known in the 13th century, but was not generally used in Britain until the great success of Bellini's opera *Norma* (1831) brought the name into popular favour. It is still fairly common. It has been used as a feminine counterpart of NORMAN.

NORMAN *m.* (naw′men)

from the Old English meaning 'from the north'. It was used in Britain before the Norman Conquest, and was popular until the 14th century.

It has long been common in Scotland, and for a while was considered a purely Scottish name, being used as a substitute for the Gaelic **Tormod** ('protected by Thor'). It is common throughout Britain today. **Norrie** is a short form.

NORRIS *m.* (*nor'is*)

from the French, meaning 'northerner'. It was originally used to describe the Vikings, and became known in Britain after the Norman Conquest. It is not common in the 20th century. It shares **Norrie** as a short form with Norman.

NOWELL *see* NOEL

NUALA *see* FENELLA

NYE *see* ANEURIN

NYGELL *see* NIGEL

O

OBADIAH *m.* (ōbedī'e)

from the Hebrew, meaning 'serving the Lord'
and the name of an Old Testament Hebrew
prophet. It became fairly common in the 17th
century when the Puritans adopted many of
these less well-known Bible names. It fell out
of favour in the 19th century.

OBERON *see* **AUBREY**

OCTAVIA *f.*, **OCTAVIUS** *m.* (oktā'vie,
oktā'vies)

from a Roman family or clan name, derived
from the Latin, meaning 'eighth'. It was also
used as a given name for an eighth child, and
is much rarer today than it was in the 19th
century. **Octavian** is an alternative masculine
form.

ODETTE, ODILE *see* **OTTILIE**

ODYSSEUS *see* **ULYSSES**

OLAF *see* **OLIVER**

OLGA *f. (ol'ge)*

from the Norse word *helga*, meaning 'holy'. The founder of the Russian monarchy is supposed to have been a Scandinavian traveller, and it was in Russia that Olga evolved. HELGA is used in Scandinavia. St Olga was the wife of the Duke of Kiev in the 10th century, and she helped spread Christianity in Russia. Olga came to England with other Russian names in the 19th century.

OLIVE, OLIVIA *f. (ol'iv, oliv'ie)*

from the Latin *oliva*, meaning 'olive'. St **Oliva** was venerated as the protectress of the olive crops in Italy. The name was first found in England in the early 13th century. Shakespeare used Olivia in *Twelfth Night* (1600), giving it some contemporary vogue and a revival in the 18th and 19th centuries. It was used again by Oliver Goldsmith in *The Vicar of Wakefield* (1766). Both forms are still used.

OLIVER *m. (ol'ive)*

The modern use of this name is derived from the French for an olive tree. It was the name of one of the most famous of Charlemagne's peers. However, the name may go back further and be connected with the Norse **Olaf**, 'remains of his ancestors'. Oliver was popular until the parliamentary revolution led by Oliver Cromwell in the 17th century, after which the name fell out of favour. It was revived in the 19th century and became quite common. **Ol** and **Ollie** are short forms. **Havelock** is said to be the Welsh form of the name.

OLWEN, OLWYN *f.* (*ol'win*)

from the Welsh, meaning 'white foot-print'. This name first occurs in the old Celtic legend in which Olwen, a giant's daughter, is wooed by a prince, who has to enlist the aid of King Arthur to accomplish the tasks that are set him. She was named Olwen because 'white trefoils sprang up wherever she trod'. The name became very popular in Wales, and spread to England in 1849 when a new translation of the *Mabinogion*, a collection of Celtic legends, was published.

ONUPHRIOS *see* HUMPHREY

OONA, OONAGH *see* UNA

OPHELIA f. (ōfē'lie)

from the Greek, meaning 'help'. It appears to have been adopted by an early 16th-century writer, but its modern use is largely due to the fame of Shakespeare's play *Hamlet* (1601). In the play, Ophelia is the girl who loves Hamlet and who eventually goes mad and is drowned.

ORESTES see ORIN

ORIANA f. (oriä'ne)

from the Latin for 'dawn'. This name is first recorded in the 16th century, when madrigal writers used it as a name for Queen Elizabeth I. The name was revived in the 19th century, and Tennyson wrote a poem called *The Ballad of Oriana*. It is rarely used today.

ORIN, ORRIN m. (or'in)

Orin was a name created by Eugene O'Neill for his play *Mourning Becomes Electra* (1931), apparently as a modern equivalent of the Greek name **Orestes**, which means 'mountaineer'. It has recently come into use, usually in the form Orrin.

ORLANDO m. (awlan'dō)

This is the Italian form of ROLAND. Italian names were fashionable in the 16th century, and Shakespeare used this one in his play *As You Like It* (1600). It was the name of a very well-known 20th-century novel by Virginia Woolf, and it is still found occasionally.

ORSON m. (aw'sen)

from the Old French Ourson, meaning 'little bear'. This is not a common name, though it is familiar through Orson Welles (1915-85), the American actor and director.

ORVILLE m. (aw'vil)

from the Old French, meaning 'golden town'. It is a fairly rare name in Britain. A famous example was Orville Wright, the aviation pioneer.

OSBERT m. (oz'bet)

from the Old English, meaning 'godbright'. It survived until the 19th century, when it became quite popular. Two well-known 20th-century bearers of the name were the writer

Osbert Sitwell and the cartoonist Osbert Lancaster, but it is now out of fashion. **Oz** and **Ozzy** are used as pet forms.

OSCAR m. (os'ke)

from the Old English **Osgar**, meaning 'godspear'. It was in use before the Norman Conquest, but seems to have died out soon after. In the 1760s James Macpherson gave the name to Ossian's son in his poems, and Napoleon's enthusiasm for the Ossianic legend caused him to give the name Oscar to his godson, later King of Sweden. It became widespread on the Continent, and in the last hundred years it has been regularly used in England and Ireland. The public disgrace of the author and playwright Oscar Wilde in 1895 caused a fall in the name's popularity.

OSWALD m. (oz'weld)

from the Old English, meaning 'god power'. Oswald, King of Northumbria in the 7th century, was killed fighting the Welsh at Oswestry. He was later canonized, and the place took its name from him. A second St Oswald helped St Dunstan with his church reforms in the 10th century. Because of these two saints, the name was popular in the Middle

Ages and has never entirely died out. **Oz** and **Ozzy** are used as pet forms.

OTTILIE *f.* (*ot'ili*)

This is the usual modern form of **Ottilia**, which is derived from the Old German meaning 'girl (or woman) of the fatherland'. St Ottilie is the patron saint of Alsace. **Ottoline** is another form of the name, and the French **Odette** and **Odile** have also been used in Britain.

OWEN, OWAIN *m.* (*ō'win*)

This is one of the most popular of all Welsh names, but its origin is uncertain. It may have come from the Latin Eugenius, meaning 'well-born', or Welsh *oen*, meaning 'lamb'. It may also be the same as EWEN, and hence mean 'a youth'. There are many bearers of the name in Welsh history and legend, but the best known is Owen Glendower, who fought for Welsh independence in the 15th century. The name has spread to the rest of Britain and to North America.

OZ(ZY) *see* OSBERT, OSWALD

P

PADDY *see* **PATRICK, PATRICIA**

PALOMA *f.* (*palō'me*)

means 'dove', the symbol of peace. Its use by
the artist Picasso for his daughter made the
name more widely known, and it is sometimes
used by admirers in memory of him.

PAMELA *f.* (*pam'ele*)

from the Greek, meaning 'all honey'. This
name dates only from the late 16th century
when it was coined by Sir Philip Sydney for
his romance *Arcadia*. It did not come into general use until the publication of Samuel Richardson's novel *Pamela* (1740). It has been most
used in the 20th century, and **Pam** is the usual
pet form. The original pronunciation, which is
no longer used, was *pamē'le*.

PANSY *f.* (*pan'ze*)

the flower used as a first name. It comes from
the French *pensée*, meaning 'a thought'.

PASCAL *m.*, **PASCALE** *f.* (*pascal'*)

a French name, meaning 'Easter', which has come into this country since the 1960s.

PATSY, PAT *see* **PATRICIA, PATRICK**

PAT, PATTY *see* **PATRICIA**

PATIENCE *f.* (*pā'shens*)

This name was fashionable in the 17th century when girls were named after abstract virtues. Sir Thomas Carew called his four daughters Patience, Temperance, Silence and Prudence. It dropped out of popular use in the 19th century, but it is still occasionally found.

PATRICIA *f.* (*petrish'e*)

the feminine of Latin *patricius*, meaning 'nobleman'.. It was originally only used in Latin records to distinguish a bearer of the name Patrick who was female, but it was used independently from the 18th century. It has become common only in the last hundred years, owing to the popularity of Queen Victoria's granddaughter Princess Patricia of Connaught. Current abbreviations are **Pat**,

Patti(e), **Patty**, **Paddy** and **Tricia** (*trish'e*)
(*see* PATRICK).

PATRICK *m.* (*pat'rik*)

from the Latin meaning 'nobleman'. St Patrick
adopted this name at his ordination. He was
born in Scotland in the late 4th century but
was captured by pirates when still a boy and
sold as a slave in Ireland. Although he escaped,
he wished to convert the Irish to Christianity,
so, after training as a missionary in France,
he returned to devote his life to this cause. The
Irish thought his name too sacred for use until
about the 17th century, and it became common
first in Scotland in the Middle Ages, whence it
spread to the North of England. In Scotland
Peter and Patrick were interchangeable right
up to the late 19th century. **Pat** and **Paddy**
are short forms, the latter being used as a
generic term for an Irishman.

PAUL *m.* (*pawl*)

from the Latin *paulus*, meaning 'small'. The
New Testament tells how Saul of Tarsus
adopted this name after his conversion. The
name was not common until the 17th century.
It was often coupled with the name Peter, as
the saints Peter and Paul share a feast day. A

notable example of this was Sir Peter Paul Rubens, the 17th-century painter. Paul became more popular after the Reformation, Peter having fallen into disfavour. Paul Jones was a Scottish Admiral who served in the American navy during the American War of Independence, and there is a popular dance named after him. The name does not occur much in English literature, but it is fairly common today.

PAULA, PAULINA, PAULINE *f.* (*paw'le̱*, *pawle̱'ne̱*, *paw'lēn*)

These are feminine derivatives of the Latin *paulus* (*see* PAUL). There was a 4th-century St Paula who founded several convents in Bethlehem, and thus gave the name some vogue in the Middle Ages. Paulina and Pauline or **Paulette** are respectively the Latin and French forms. Pauline has been more often used in modern times, though there are signs that Paula is superseding it. **Polly** is sometimes used as a pet form.

PEARL *f.* (*pe̱l*)

This name first became common in the 19th century, with other gem names (*see* BERYL, RUBY). It has also been used as a pet name for

MARGARET, which is derived from the Greek for 'pearl'. There is a 14th-century Middle English poem about a little girl called Pearl where the name is probably allegorical. In America it has occasionally been used as a man's name.

PEG, PEGGY see MARGARET

PELAGIUS see MORGAN

PENELOPE f. (p̲enel'ōpi)

from the Greek. The first element may be *pene*, meaning 'bobbin'. In Homer's *Odyssey*, it was the name of Odysseus' wife, who waited ten years for her husband to return from the Trojan War. The name has been used regularly, though infrequently, since the 16th century. It has been more popular in Ireland where it is used as an equivalent of the native FENELLA. It is often abbreviated to **Pen** or **Penny**.

PEPPI see PERPETUA

PERCEVAL, PERCIVAL m. (pe'sivel)

The origin of this name is obscure. It has been suggested that it is a combination of French *perce* and *val*, meaning 'pierce valley'. When used as a surname, Perceval probably referred to Percheval, a place in Normandy. The name has been used in this country since the 14th century but is not common. The short forms are **Perce** or PERCY, and sometimes **Val**.

PERCY m. (*pe'si*)

This famous northern family is descended from William de Perci, one of William the Conqueror's companions, who took his name from a village in Normandy (*see* PERCEVAL). At first its use as a Christian name was confined to connections of the Percy family, but during the 19th century it came into general use, probably partly due to the poet, Percy Bysshe Shelley. It shares the short form **Perce** with Perceval.

PERDITA f. (*pe'dite*)

This is the feminine of the Latin *perditus*, meaning 'lost'. It was coined by Shakespeare for the heroine of *A Winter's Tale* (1611). It has been used as a direct result of this.

PEREGRINE m. (*per'egrin*)

from the Latin *peregrinus*, meaning 'stranger' or 'traveller' and hence 'pilgrim'. There was a

7th-century saint of this name who was a hermit near Modena in Italy. The name has been used in this country since about the 13th century, but it has always been rather uncommon. PERRY is used as a short form.

PERPETUA f. (*pepet'ūe*)

from the Latin, meaning 'everlasting' or 'perpetual'. The name is used mostly in commemoration of a 3rd-century Christian martyr. A diminutive is **Peppi**.

PERRY m. (*per'i*)

This name sometimes occurs as an abbreviation of PEREGRINE, but it is also a surname used as a first name. It was the surname of two 19th-century American admirals, one of whom inflicted a defeat on the British while the other led the expedition that opened up Japan to the west. Their exploits probably encouraged the use of the name in the US. The singer Perry Como, who helped spread the popularity of the name, was born Pierino.

PETER m. (*pē'ter*)

from the Greek *petras*, meaning 'rock'. Cephas is the Aramaic equivalent which Jesus gave as a nickname to Simon bar Jonah, to be symbolic of steadfastness in faith. Peter was chief of the Apostles and became the first Bishop of Rome. He was the favourite saint of the medieval church and his name was very popular throughout Christendom in the Middle Ages. In England the name is first recorded in Domesday Book in the Latin form **Petrus**. The Normans brought over the French form **Piers** which was usual until the 14th century, when Peter became predominant. It was unfashionable after the Reformation because of its association with the Papacy, and was later thought of as a rustic name. It did not return to fashion until 1904, when James Barrie's *Peter Pan* was published, but it is now one of the most popular boys' names. A short form is **Pete**. **Peta** and **Petra** are 20th-century feminine forms of the name.

PETRONELLA, PETRONILLA *f.*
(*petrōnel'e, petrōnil'e*)

These are feminine diminutives of Petronius, the Roman family name which may originally have come from *petra*, meaning 'stone'. Petronilla was thought, erroneously, to have been the name of St Peter's daughter, and because of this the name was popular in the Middle Ages.

It was used as the feminine equivalent of Peter.

PETULA f. (petu'le)

from the Latin, meaning 'seeker'. It is uncommon in Britain, but the singer Petula Clark has made the name better known.

PHILIP m. (fil'ip)

from the Greek meaning 'lover of horses'. It was common in the Middle Ages, on account of the Apostle of that name. In Elizabeth I's reign Philip of Spain was the arch enemy of England, and the name suffered accordingly. It was revived in the 19th century and is now common, the best known bearer at present being Prince Philip, Duke of Edinburgh. **Phil** is now the most usual short form, although **Pip** and **Flip** are sometimes used. **Phillip** is a variant spelling which reflects the form usually found in surnames.

PHILIPPA f. (fil'ipe)

This is the feminine form of PHILIP, but originally only used to distinguish women named Philip, in Latin records. Its use as a separate name dates from about the 19th century. It is now quite popular and is often abbreviated to **Pippa**, an Italian form.

PHILLIS *see* PHYLLIS

PHOEBE *f.* (*fē'bi*)

from the Greek, meaning 'the shining one'. It is one of the titles given by the Greeks to their moon goddess. It occurs in St Paul's Epistle to the Romans and, perhaps for this reason, was adopted after the Reformation, reaching its peak of popularity in the 17th century. It is still found, but is not popular.

PHYLLIS, PHILLIS *f.* (*fil'is*)

from the Greek, meaning 'leafy'. In Greek legend it was the name of a girl who died for love and was transformed into an almond tree. It was used as a name for country girls in pastoral poetry and so became unfashionable until its 19th century revival. **Phyllida** is an alternative form which is sometimes found.

PIA *f.* (*pē'e*)

from the Latin, meaning 'pious'. This name has recently been given some publicity by the starlet Pia Zadora.

PIERS *see* **PETER**

PIPPA *see* **PHILIPPA**

POLLY *see* **PAULINE, MARY**

POPPY *f.* (*po'pē*)
___

the flower used as a name. It was particularly popular at the end of the last century and the beginning of this, but is still in use.

PRIMROSE *f.* (*prim'rōs*)
___

This flower name was popular at the beginning of the 20th century. Earlier examples in the 18th century probably derived from the Scottish surname.

PRISCILLA *f.* (*prisil'e*)
___

This is the Latin diminutive of *prisca*, meaning 'ancient'. It was the name of a woman mentioned in the Acts of the Apostles. She was the wife of the Roman Jew Aquila, (Acts XVIII.2.). As with other New Testament names it was a favourite with the 17th-century Puritans. It also appears as **Prisca** but this form is obsolete. **Pris** and **Prissy** are sometimes found as short forms, but **Cilla** is the most used.

PRUDENCE f. ($pr\acute{o}\acute{o}'d\underline{e}ns$)

Prudence first appears in Chaucer, and it was one of the first abstract virtues to be adopted as a name by the Puritans. It is one of the few to have survived in use to the present day, and is now usually abbreviated to **Prue**.

PRUNELLA f. ($pr\acute{o}\acute{o}nel'\underline{e}$)

from the French, meaning 'prune-coloured'. It is also the name of a kind of silk and the Latin name for a wild flower, the self-heal, and a bird, the hedge sparrow or dunnock. The actress Prunella Scales has made the name more widely known.

Q

QUEENIE f. (kwē′ni)

This name is sometimes given independently, but it is really a pet name for **Regina**, which is Latin for 'queen'. The latter was used from the Middle Ages, possibly with reference to the Virgin Mary, Queen of Heaven. Queenie was also used as a nickname for girls christened Victoria during Queen Victoria's long reign.

QUENTIN, QUINTIN m. (kwen′tin, kwin′tin)

from the Roman clan Quintian, whose simple way of life made them famous among the lavish Romans. Quentin was the French form which the Normans introduced to England. It became obsolete after the Middle Ages except in Scotland. Its revival in the 19th century was probably due to Sir Walter Scott's historical romance *Quentin Durward* (1823). It may also have been used occasionally as a given name for a fifth child. **Quinton** is another form of the name.

QUINCY *m.* (*kwin'si*)

a surname taken from a French place name.
Its use in the United States is principally due
to the influence of John Quincy Adams (1767-
1848), the country's sixth President.

R

RAB, RABBIE *see* **ROBERT**

RACHEL *f.* (*rā'chel*)

from the Hebrew for 'ewe', which was symbolic
of gentleness and innocence. In the Book of
Genesis Rachel was the daughter of Laban
who was 'beautiful and well-favoured', and for
whose hand Jacob served seven years (Gen.
XXIX.20.). In Britain the name was adopted
after the Reformation, and it was very popular
in the 17th and 19th centuries. The usual pet
forms today are **Rach**, **Rachie**, **Rae** and **Ray**.
The actress **Raquel** Welch shows the Spanish
form of the name. From Rachel have developed
the forms **Rachelle** (sometimes pronounced
rashel') and **Rochelle**, the French word for 'a
small rock', and the name of a town in
Brittany. They have SHELLEY as a short form.

RADULF *see* **RALPH**

RAE, RAY *see* **RACHEL, RAYMOND**

RAFF, RAUF *see* **RALPH**

RALPH *m. (ralf', rāf)*

from the Old Norse, meaning 'counsel wolf'. In the earlier form, **Radulf**, this name was fairly common in England before the Norman Conquest, and it was reinforced by the French use. The medieval spellings were **Ralf**, **Rauf** and **Raff**(e) which were pronounced *rāf*. Ralf occurs from the 16th century, **Rafe** was the common form in the 17th century and Ralph appears in the 18th century. These names were all pronounced *rāf* until quite recently, when there has been a return to the earlier *ralf* (*see* RAOUL, ROLF).

RANALD *see* **RONALD**

RANDOLPH *m. (ran'dolf)*

from the Old English Randwulf, meaning 'shield wolf', which in the Middle Ages became **Ranulf** and **Randal**(l). The latter was latinized as **Randulfus**, and it was from this form that Randolph was coined in the 18th century. The short form **Randy** has been used as a name in its own right, particularly in the US.

RAOUL *m.* (*rawl'*, *ra'óól*)

This is the French equivalent of RALPH, derived
from **Radulf**. It was used in Britain after the
Norman Conquest, but died out with the
decline of French speaking in this country. It
has been used occasionally in the 20th century
(e.g. the US film director Raoul Walsh), possibly because of the large number of soldiers
who fought in France in two World Wars.

RAQUEL *see* RACHEL

RASTUS *see* ERASTUS

RAYMOND *m.* (*rā'mend*)

from the Old German, meaning 'counsel
protection'. The Normans brought the name
to Britain and it was particularly popular in
crusading times. Two 13th-century saints bore
the name. One of them spent much of his life
rescuing Spaniards captured by the Moors.
Today the name is more popular than ever
before. Its abbreviation **Ray** is sometimes
given independently. There is a feminine **Ray-
monde** which also has the short forms Ray
and **Rae**.

REBECCA f. (<u>rebek</u>'e)

In Hebrew this means a 'noose' or 'knotted cord' and since this has the quality of not being able to slip, it came to mean a 'faithful wife'. In the Old Testament Rebekah was the wife of Isaac, and was renowned for her beauty. It was a favourite name among the Puritans, who took it to North America. Daphne du Maurier's classic novel *Rebecca*, which was an equally popular film, may have done something towards reviving the name. **Becky** is the short form.

REDMOND m. (red'mend)

from the Old English, meaning 'counsel protector'. It is rarely found in Britain.

REG, REGGIE see **REGINALD**

REGINA see **QUEENIE**

REGINALD m. (rej'ineld)

This name has the same origin as REYNOLD and appears first as **Reginaldus**, a latinized form of this name. Reginald appears in the 15th century and seems to have started as a more formal alternative to Reynold. Neither name was common between the 15th and 19th centuries, but Reginald was then revived and became very common. It can be abbreviated to **Reg**, **Reggie** or **Rex** (*see* RONALD).

REINALD *see* REYNOLD

RENÉ(E) *m. and f.* (*re̱'nā̱*)

These are French names derived from the Latin *renatus*, meaning 'reborn'. The Latin form was sometimes used by Puritans in the 17th century, and the French forms have been used in Britain in the 20th century. The Latin feminine form **Renata** is still used occasionally. The name can also be spelt **Rennie** and **Renny**.

RENIE *see* IRENE

REUBEN *m.* (*ró̱ó̱'be̱n*)

from the Hebrew, meaning 'behold a son'. In Biblical times it was sometimes given to the son born to replace a child who had died, and it appears in the Bible as the name of a son of Jacob. The form **Ruben** is also found (*see* RUFUS).

REX *m.* *(reks)*

This is the Latin for 'king' which has only been used as a first name in recent times. It is also found as an abbreviation of REGINALD and ERIC.

REYNARD *m.* *(re'nàd)*

from the Old German, meaning 'mighty and brave'. This and **Rainard** were the Norman French forms, but they never became as common as Reynold, with which they were often confused. It is very rare today, except as a term for a fox.

REYNOLD *m.* *(ren'eld)*

from the Old English **Regenweald**, meaning 'power force'. This was not a common Anglo-Saxon name, but it was reinforced at the time of the Norman Conquest by the French equivalent **Reinald**, or **Reynaud**. It was quite common up to the 15th century, by which time REGINALD was superseding it (*see* RONALD).

RHIANNON *f.* *(rēan'on)*

the name of an important figure in medieval Welsh literature. There is evidence that she was originally a Celtic goddess connected with horses. The name means 'nymph, goddess' and is mainly confined to Wales.

RHODA *f.* (rō'de)

Derived from the Greek for 'rose', this is a New Testament name (Acts X.11-13.), that was taken into use in the 17th century.

RHODRI *see* RODERICK

RHONA, RONA *see* ROWENA

RHONDA *f.* (ron'de)

a simplified spelling of the Welsh place name Rhondda, which has been used as a first name since the early part of this century.

RHONWEN *see* ROWENA

RHYS *m.* (rēs')

a common Welsh name meaning 'rashness'. The popularity of this name is due to the ancient Welsh family of this name. A Prince Rhys checked the Norman advance into Wales, and his grandson was appointed by Henry II as his Welsh deputy. It was a man called Rhys ap Thomas who had the power in Wales to establish Henry VII's dominion over it.

RIA *see* MARY

RICHARD *m.* (rich'ed)

This name first appears in Anglo-Saxon as **Ricehard**, meaning 'a hard ruler', which was later developed into **Ricard**. It was the Normans who spread the present form of the name, the softer, French, Richard. Richard Coeur-de-Lion's fame as a crusader gave the name great popularity, which was only slightly subdued by the bad reputations of the second and third English kings of this name. The short form **Dick** appears as early as the 13th century, and this is still very common, though **Rich**(ie), **Dickie**, **Rick**(ie), **Dickon** and many others, have been used at various times. Richard is one of the commonest boys' names in Britain today.

RICK, RICKIE *see* RICHARD, DEREK, ERIC, FREDERICK

RITA *f.* (rē′te)

an abbreviation of Margarita (*see* MARGARET). It is also used as a separate name, and may have been popularized in the 20th century by the film star Rita Hayworth (1918-87).

ROBERT m. (rob'et)

This name is derived from the Old German, meaning 'fame bright'. Although there was an equivalent Anglo-Saxon name, it was the French form which took hold in Britain after the Norman Conquest. Robert the Bruce popularized the name in Scotland where it has the local short forms **Rab** and **Rabbie**. **Bob**, **Bobbie** and **Bert** are used in England. **Robin** was a French diminutive of **Rob**, which came to Britain in the Middle Ages, and is now equally popular as a name in its own right.

ROBERTA, ROBINA f. (rebert'e, rebēn'e)

These are feminine forms of ROBERT and Robin. Both have been popular, mainly in Scotland. Oliver Cromwell's sister was called Robina. BOBBIE and **Robin** or **Robyn** have become popular names derived from them.

ROBIN, ROBYN see ROBERT, ROBERTA

ROCHELLE see RACHEL

RODERICK *m.* (*rod'erik*)

from the Old German, meaning 'fame rule'.
The Goths took the name to Spain where it
became **Rodrigo**, and it was established there
at least as early as the 8th century. In Britain
the name is most common in Scotland where
it was originally used to transliterate a Gaelic
name **Ruaridh** (*see* RORY), meaning 'red'. In
Wales it is used as a modern equivalent of the
Welsh **Rhodri**, meaning 'crown ruler'. Short
forms are **Rod** and **Roddy**.

RODGE *see* ROGER

RODNEY *m.* (*rod'ni*)

This means 'reed island', and was originally a
surname taken from the name of the Somerset
village Rodney Stoke. It was not used as a
Christian name until Admiral George Rodney
gave it heroic associations in the 18th century.
Since then it has become widespread. Short
forms are **Rod** and **Roddy**.

RODRIGO *see* RODERICK

ROGER *m.* (*roj'e*)

Hrothgar, meaning 'fame spear', was an
Anglo-Saxon name, but it was the Normans

who gave us the present form, which was derived from an Old German equivalent. Roger was a favourite name in the Middle Ages. From the 16th to the 19th centuries it was mainly a peasant name, but today it is widespread and more common than ever. The ancient short form **Hodge**, once a type-name for a farm labourer, has been replaced by **Rodge**.

ROLAND, ROWLAND m. (rō'lend)

from the Old German **Hrodland**, meaning 'fame land'. Roland was the most famous of Charlemagne's peers, and it was the Normans who brought the name to England in this form. The ballad of *Childe Rowland*, an old story about a son of King Arthur, shows the usual spelling of the name up to the 19th century. It was very common in the Middle Ages owing to its literary association, particulary the *Chanson de Roland*, a 12th century French epic. ORLANDO is the Italian version which was popular in the 15th and 16th centuries. Roland is still very popular today.

ROLF m. (rolf)

from the Old German, meaning 'fame wolf'. This name developed in Normandy and came to Britain at the time of the Norman Conquest. It was quite soon absorbed into RALPH, but was revived in the late 19th century and is still current. **Rollo** is a latinization. Rollo the Ganger ('Walker') was a 9th-century Norwegian exile who, with his followers, founded the Norman race.

ROMY *see* ROSEMARY

RONA *see* ROWENA

RONALD *m.* (ron'eld)

Ronald and **Ranald** are Scottish equivalents of REYNOLD and REGINALD, but they are of Norse not Old English derivation. Ranald is still exclusively Scottish but Ronald is now widespread. Diminutive forms commonly used are **Ron** and **Ronnie**.

RORY, RORIE *m.* (raw'ri)

from the Celtic **Ruairidh**, meaning 'red'. The name became popular in Ireland due to the fame of the 12th-century King Rory O'Connor. It is also widely used in the Scottish Highlands, and is sometimes used in England as an abbreviation of RODERICK.

ROSA *see* **ROSE**

ROSABEL, ROSABELLA, ROSALBA *see* **ROSE**

ROSALIE f. (*roz'eli, rōz'eli*)

probably from Latin *rosalia*. This is the name of a Roman festival, when garlands of roses were draped on tombs. Its use as a Christian name is due to St **Rosalia**, a 12th-century hermit, the patron saint of Palermo in Sicily. **Rosalie** is the French form and **Rosaleen** the Irish.

ROSALIND f. (*roz'elind*)

The origin of this name is the Old German **Roslindis**, meaning 'horse serpent'. When the Goths took it to Spain it was interpreted as *rosa* and *linda*, 'pretty rose', and it was with this meaning that it came over to Britain in Elizabeth I's reign. It was used by Shakespeare for the heroine of *As You Like It* (1600) and in another form, **Rosaline**, in two other plays. Largely due to this romantic literary association, it has been popular ever since.

ROSAMUND, ROSAMOND f. (*roz'emend*)

from the Old German, meaning 'horse protection'. It has generally been associated with the Latin *rosa munda*, meaning 'pure rose'. The Normans brought the name to England and, unlike most names of Germanic origin, it survived the Renaissance. It was usually spelt Rosamond in the French fashion, but both forms are used today. **Rose** is used as a short form of both this name and ROSALIND.

ROSE *f.* (rōz)

This is the most popular of all flower names which are used as personal names, but it has an older and quite different derivation. Its source is the Old German *hros*, meaning 'horse' (*see* ROSALIND, ROSAMUND). The name was brought to England by the Normans, and it has been consistently popular, giving rise to many derivatives, like **Rosalba**, 'white rose', **Rosetta**, 'little rose', and **Rosabel(la)**, 'beautiful rose', as well as **Rosanna**, **Rosina**, **Rosita** and the pet form **Rosie**. **Rosa** is a Latin form which has been used occasionally since the 19th century.

ROSEMARY *f.* (rōz'meri)

This is generally considered to be a borrowed plant name, although it is sometimes thought of as a combination of ROSE and MARY. The plant name is derived from the Latin *ros* and *marinus*, meaning 'dew' and 'of the sea'. It was probably first used in 1745 and was for a long time confined to one family. But in the 20th century it has become widespread and very popular. It can be spelt **Rosemarie**. **Roma**, **Romy** and **Rosie** are short forms.

ROSLINDIS *see* ROSALIND

ROSS *m.* (ros)

from the Gaelic, meaning 'of the peninsula', the name of a famous Scottish clan. It is popular in Scotland.

ROWAN *m.* (rō'w<u>e</u>n)

from the Irish **Ruadhan**, meaning 'little red-(haired) one'. It was the name of an Irish saint. The comedian Rowan Atkinson is a well-known example of the name.

ROWENA *f.* (rōe'ne)

from the Welsh **Rhonwen**, meaning 'slender fair' or 'fair lance'. There was a Rowena in the 5th century, the daughter of the Jutish ruler Hengist, who fell in love with Vortigern, a Celtic chieftain. Its modern use is due to Sir

Walter Scott, who gave the name to the heroine of his novel *Ivanhoe* (1819). Variant forms are **Rowina** and **Rhona** or **Rona**, although this is also the name of two Scottish islands.

ROWLAND see ROLAND

ROXANA, ROXANE, ROXANNE *f.*
(*roks'ane, roksan'*)

These are anglicized forms of the Persian **Raokshna**, which means 'brilliant one'. Roxana was the name of Alexander the Great's wife.

ROY *m.* (*roi*)

from the Gaelic *ruadh*, meaning 'red'. This name is often mistakenly thought to derive from the French word for 'king'. A well-known example of the name is the famous Highlander, Robert Macgregor, commonly known as Rob Roy because of his red hair, who was involved in the Jacobite Rising of 1715. In the 20th century it is well known in all English-speaking countries. Sir Walter Scott's novel *Rob Roy* (1817), may have contributed to its popularity.

ROZ see ROSAMUND

RUBEN *see* **REUBEN**

RUBY *f. (rŏŏ'bi)*

This is one of many jewel names that were taken into use during the 19th century.

RUDOLF, RUDOLPH *m. (rŏŏ'dolf)*

from the Old German **Hrodulf**, meaning 'fame wolf'. Rudolf is the Modern German form of the name which has only been used in this country for about a hundred years. Earlier examples occurred only among German immigrants. The spread of this name was undoubtedly helped by the widespread adoration of Rudolf Valentino (1895-1926), the American film star. Another American, the singer **Rudy** Vallee (1901-86) made the pet form well known.

RUDYARD *m. (rud'iàd)*

from an Old English place name, possibly meaning 'red enclosure'. This name is best known for Rudyard Kipling (1865-1936), the great writer on India. Kipling was christened Rudyard after the lake in Staffordshire, where his parents had first met.

RUFUS m. (rŏŏ'fes)

This is a Latin word meaning 'red-haired'. William Rufus was the second son of William the Conqueror, and became King William II of England. The name has been used as an English equivalent of REUBEN.

RUPERT m. (rŏŏ'pet)

This name has the same origin as ROBERT and means 'bright fame'. It developed in Germany, where it became **Rupprecht**, and Rupert is an English transliteration. Rupert of the Rhine was Charles I's nephew and a brilliant general and a scientist. He came to England to support the Royalist cause and was much admired for his dashing bravery. It was because of him that the English form was coined and became popular. An equally romantic figure in modern times was the poet Rupert Brooke, who died in the First World War aged 27.

RUSSELL m. (rus'el)

This is primarily a surname and is derived from the French *rousseile*, which means 'little red one'. It came into use as a first name along with other famous family names in the 19th century. **Rus(s)** and **Rusty** are pet forms.

RUTH *f.* (*rŏŏth*)

from the Hebrew, possibly meaning 'vision of beauty'. It was a common name just after the Reformation on account of the Old Testament heroine who gave her name to the *Book of Ruth*. The qualities attached to Ruth in the Bible are faithfulness and devotion. The name was also associated with the abstract noun, ruth, meaning 'sorrow' or 'pity'. It is still used fairly frequently, with **Ruthie** as a pet form.

RYAN *m.* (*rī'en*)

a common Irish surname, of unknown meaning, now a very popular first name. Its popularity was greatly helped by the success of the film star Ryan O'Neal (b. 1941).

S

SABIN(A) m. and f. (sab'in, sabēn'e)

Sabinus and Sabina are Latin names meaning respectively a Sabine man and woman. These have survived in England as Sabin and Sabina on account of two early saints who bore the name. Only the feminine form has survived as a Christian name; it is rarely used. There is also a French form, **Sabine**.

SABRINA f. (sebrēn'e)

from the Latin, meaning 'from the boundary line', and the Latin name of the river Severn. Milton used it for the spirit of the river in his play *Camus*.

SACHA m. and f. (sa'she)

originally a Russian short form of ALEXANDER. The name was given publicity by the French singer Sacha Distel. Although basically a man's name, it is sometimes used for women. **Sasha** is an alternative form.

SACHEVERELL *m. (seshev'erel)*

This is an old family name. It has been suggested that it originated as a Norman nickname, *Sans Cheverel*, meaning 'without leather'. Its use as a Christian name dated from the early 18th century when a Dr Sacheverell was a Tory preacher. The best-known example in this century is Sacheverell Sitwell, the writer, but the name is not now in general use.

SADIE *see* SARAH

SAFFRON *f. (saf'ren)*

the name of the golden-yellow spice and of the crocus it comes from, used as a first name.

SAIREY, SAREY *see* SARAH

SAL, SALLY *see* SARAH

SALAMON *see* SOLOMON

SALLY *f.* (*sal'i*)

originally a pet name for SARAH, but nowadays used separately.

SALOME *f.* (*selōm'i, sa'lōmā*)

This is the Greek form of an Aramaic name meaning 'peace of Zion'. In the New Testament it is the name of one of the women who looked after Jesus, and was the first person at his tomb on Easter Sunday. This led to its use in Britain in the 17th century among Puritans. However, the most famous holder of the name was another New Testament character, Salome, daughter of Herodias, who is infamous for causing the beheading of John the Baptist, and the name is primarily associated with her story. This may be partly responsible for its unpopularity today.

SAM *see* **SAMUEL**

SAMANTHA *f.* (*seman'the*)

may be from Aramaic, meaning 'a listener', but is probably a 17th-century coinage, meant to be a feminine version of SAMUEL. It has been popular since the 1950s, when it was used for

one of the characters in the film *High Society*
and appeared in a song title.

SAM(P)SON *m.* (*sam'sen*)

from the Hebrew, meaning 'child of the sun'.
In the Old Testament, Samson was a judge,
and champion of the Israelites against the
Philistines. He was famous for his great
strength. The Normans brought the name to
England, and the French spelling **Sanson** was
also used. The name continued in use until the
17th century but thereafter became unusual.

SAMUEL *m.* (*sam'ūel*)

from the Hebrew, meaning 'heard by God' or
'asked by God'. The two Books of Samuel in
the Old Testament tell how the prophet was
the leader of the Israelites until they
demanded a king, how he had to anoint Saul,
and later trained David to replace him. In
Scotland and Ireland it was for a long time
used to transliterate the Gaelic **Somhairle**, a
name derived from Old Norse and meaning
'summer wanderer', or 'Viking'. Its short forms
are **Sam** and **Sammy**, and SAMANTHA is probably a feminine form.

SANCHIA f. (san'chie)

This is a Provencal and Spanish name derived from the Latin *sanctus*, meaning 'holy'. The name came to England in the 13th century when the Earl of Cornwall married Sanchia, daughter of the Count of Provence. The name then took many forms including **Sence**, **Science** and **Saint**. The original form survived and is still used occasionally.

SANDRA f. (sàn'dre, san'dre)

This is a short form of Italian **Alessandra**, now used as a name in its own right (*see* ALEXANDRA). **Sandie** or **Sandy** are pet forms, and the designer **Zandra** Rhodes uses an unusual alternative form.

SANDY see ALEXANDER

SANSON see SAMSON

SARA(H) f. (se're, sā're)

from the Hebrew, meaning 'princess', and the name of Abraham's wife in the Old Testament. This name was not common until the Reformation but it was very popular in the 17th and 18th centuries. During this period it was familiarly rendered **Sarey** or **Sairey**, e.g. Dickens' character in *Martin Chuzzlewit*, Sairey Gamp, who always carried a bulky umbrella. **Sally**, **Sal** and **Sadie** are pet forms. In Ireland Sarah has been used to render the Irish **Sorcha**, meaning 'bright', and **Saraid**, meaning 'excellent'. Sarah is a fairly common girl's name in Britain today.

SASHA *see* SACHA

SASKIA *f. (sas'kēe)*

This was the name of the wife of the Dutch artist Rembrandt (1606-69), whose paintings of her have made her famous. It may be connected with the word 'Saxon'.

SAUL *m. (sawl)*

from the Hebrew, meaning 'asked for'. This name occurs in the Old Testament as the name of the first King of Israel, and in the New Testament as St Paul's name before his conversion. It was first used as a Christian name in Britain in the 17th century, and has been used occasionally since.

SCOTT *m.* (*skot*)

This is a surname, meaning 'a Scot', used as a first name. The American writer Scott Fitzgerald (1896-1940) is a famous example.

SEAMUS *see* SHAMUS

SEAN *m.* (*shawn'*)

This is the Irish form of JOHN and developed from the French **Jean**. It is also spelt **Shaun**. The variant form **Shane** was pronounced the same way, though it has now come to be pronounced *shān*, as in the famous Western film of that name.

SEBASTIAN *m.* (*sebast'ien*)

from the Latin **Sebastianus**, meaning 'man of Sebastia'. The name of this town in Asia Minor was derived from the Greek, meaning 'majestic' or 'venerable'. St Sebastian was executed by being shot at with arrows, and his martyrdom was a particularly popular subject of medieval painting. The name took hold in Spain, and in France, where it was shortened to **Bastien**, and taken across the Channel from Brittany to the West Country by fishermen. The form **Bastian** took root there. The name did not spread to the rest of Britain until mod-ern times, but Sebastian is now reasonably common, having the short forms **Seb** and **Sebbie**.

SELENE *see* **SELINA**

SELEWINE *see* **SELWYN**

SELINA *f.* (*selē′ne*)

The etymology of this name is disputed. One possible derivation is from **Selene**, the Greek for 'moon goddess'; another from the Latin name **Coelina**, from *caelum*, meaning 'heaven', through the French form **Céline** (*sālēn*). **Celina** is found in the Middle Ages which rather confirms the second theory. The television personality Selina Scott has made the name well known.

SELWYN *m.* (*sel′win*)

possibly from the Old English *selewine*, mean-ing 'house friend'. The surname Selwyn occurs in the 13th century but its use as a first name seems to date only from the 19th century, when it became common for distinguished surnames to be used as first names by the general public.

SEPTIMUS *m.* (*sep'time̲s*)

This is the Latin word for 'seventh'. It was used as a first name in the 19th century when large families were common, though it was occasionally used out of its numerical context. **Septima** was the feminine form.

SERAPHINA *f.* (*serefē'ne̲*)

This is a Latin derivative of the Hebrew, meaning 'burning' or 'passionate one'. St Seraphina was an Italian abbess of the 15th century. The name has been used, though very rarely, since the 19th century, and is sometimes spelt **Serafina**.

SERENA *f.* (*se'rāne̲, se'rēne̲*)

This is the feminine form of the Latin *serenus*, meaning 'calm', 'serene'. Edmund Spenser used the name for a character in his epic poem *The Faerie Queene* in the late 16th century.

SEUMAS *see* **SHAMUS**

SEXTUS *m.* (*seks'te̲s*)

This is the Latin for 'sixth', and was sometimes used in the 19th century for either a sixth son or a sixth male child.

SHAMUS *m.* (shā'mus)

This is a modern phonetic version of **Seumus** or **Seamus**, which is the Irish for JAMES.

SHANE *see* SEAN

SHANNON *f.* (shan'en)

the Irish river and place name, meaning 'the old one', which has come to be used as a first name in recent years.

SHARLENE *see* CHARLENE

SHARON *f.* (sha'ren, shee'ren)

In the Bible Sharon, which means 'the plain', is an area of rich natural beauty. To compare a woman to it came to be a great compliment. It has been used as a first name only this century, but has been very popular.

SHAUN *see* SEAN

SHEILA *f.* (shē'le)

This is a phonetic spelling of the Irish name **Sile**, which was derived from Celia (*see* CECILIA). Sheila is now a popular name throughout Britain, and in Australia is used as a generic term for a young woman. In Ireland it is often spelt **Shelagh**.

SHE(E)NA *f.* (*shē'ne*)

This is a phonetic form of **Sine** which is the Gaelic for JANE. The singer Sheena Easton has made it better known. **Shona** comes from the same root.

SHELLEY *f.* (*shel'le*)

a pet form of MICHELLE and RACHEL as well as being a variant of the name SHIRLEY. From the 1940s the name was brought to public attention by the actress Shelley Winters. Its association with the Romantic poet Percy Bysshe Shelley (1792-1822) may have helped its spread.

SHEREE, SHERRIE, SHERRY *see* CHERIE

SHERLOCK *m.* (*sher'lok*)

from the Old English, meaning 'fair-haired'. This name was immortalized by Sir Arthur Conan Doyle in his detective stories about Sherlock Holmes.

SHERYL *see* **CHERYL**

SHIMEON *see* **SIMEON, SIMON**

SHIRLEY *f.* (*she'li*)

This was originally a place name meaning 'shire meadow', and from this it became a surname in Yorkshire and elsewhere. Charlotte Bronte started the fashion for it as a girls' Christian name in 1849, when her novel of that name appeared. The name became popular in the US, where the child film star Shirley Temple was born (1928). It was chiefly her admirers who made the name popular in Britain.

SHONA *see* **SHEENA**

SHUSHANNAH *see* **SUSAN**

SIAN *f.* (*shàn*)

the Welsh form of JANE. The actress Siân Phillips is a well-known user of the name.

SIBYL, SYBIL *f.* (*sib'el*)

In classical times the Sibyls were prophetesses, and some of them were supposed to have foretold the coming of Christ. Because of this,

Sibylla came to be used as a Christian name, the Normans bringing it with them to England, where it became common in several forms. Sybil had a revival in the second half of the 19th century after Disraeli had published his political novel of that name (1845). The actress **Cybill** Shepherd has introduced another form of the name.

SIDNEY, SYDNEY m. and f. (sid'ni)

This is a surname which has its origin in the French place name St Denis. A great historical character who caused the name to be taken into use as a first name was the Elizabethan soldier and poet, Sir Philip Sidney. The spelling Sydney did not appear until the 19th century, and the city in Australia was named after Viscount Sydney, who was Secretary of State at the time. The short form is **Sid**. In the 18th century girls were given surnames as first names more often than is usual today, and Sydney as a girl's name may date from this. Alternatively, it may be a form of the Latin name **Sidonia**, 'woman of Sidon', which became **Sidonie** in French and **Sidony** in English. In the US Sydney is regarded primarily as a female name.

SIEGFRIED m. (sēg'frēd)

from the Old German, meaning 'victory peace'.
It was first used in Britain at the end of the
19th century, due largely to the cult for
Wagner's music. Siegfried is the name of the
mythical hero of Wagner's opera cycle *The
Ring* (1874). Siegfried Sassoon (1886-1967)
was a famous British poet.

SILE *see* SHEILA

SILVESTER, SYLVESTER m. (silvest'e)

Silvester is Latin for 'a wood-dweller'. There
have been three popes of this name. The name
was quite common in both forms in the Middle
Ages and it has survived to the present day.
Sylvester is now the more popular of the two.
Sylvestra is a rare feminine form.

SILVIA, SYLVIA f. (sil'vie)

This is the feminine form of the Latin *Silvius*,
meaning 'of the wood'. Rhea Silvia was the
mother of Romulus and Remus, the founders
of Rome. This may have been the reason why
the name was adopted during the Renaissance

in Italy. Like other classical names, it came to England in Elizabethan times. Shakespeare used it in *Two Gentlemen of Verona* (1592), and this probably gave rise to its widespread use in Britain. The diminutive form is **Sylvie**.

SIMEON *m.* (*sim'ien*)

from the Hebrew **Shimeon**, meaning 'listening'. This has the same origin as SIMON. The translators of the Bible into English used this form in the Old Testament. In the New Testament it is the name of the old man who blessed the baby Jesus in the Temple, and first recited the Nunc Dimittis. Simeon was used in Britain in the Middle Ages and again after the Reformation, but is uncommon now.

SIMON *m.*, SIMONE *f.* (*sī'men, sēmōn'*)

This is the better-known English form of Shimeon (*see* SIMON). The popularity of Simon in the Middle Ages was due to Simon Peter, the Apostle, whose popularity was great at that period. Like PETER, it went out of fashion after the Reformation because of its Roman Catholic associations, though it is now fashionable again. Simone is a feminine form taken from the French.

SINCLAIR *m. (sin'cler)*

This is a contraction of St Clair, a town in Normandy (*see also* SIDNEY). The Normans brought the name to England and it developed as a surname, mainly in Scotland. It has been used as a first name at least since the 19th century.

SINE *see* SHEENA

SIS, SISLEY, SISSY *see* CECILIA

SOLOMON *m. (sol'emen)*

from the Hebrew, meaning 'little man of peace'. In the Old Testament King Solomon was renowned for his wisdom. The name was more often rendered **Salamon** in the Middle Ages. It died out, but was revived by Puritans after the Reformation. **Solly** is a frequently used abbreviation.

SOMHAIRLE *see* SAMUEL

SONIA *f. (son'ie)*

This is a Russian diminutive form of SOPHIA, and its use in Britain is recent, perhaps a result of the novel of this name by Stephen

McKenna, published in 1917. **Sonya** and **Sonja** are other forms of the name.

SOPHIA, SOPHIE f. (sōfi'_e, sōfē'_e, sō'fi)

from the Greek, meaning 'wisdom'. Sophia became a popular name in the Eastern Church on account of the great cathedral Hagia Sophia at Constantinople. The name spread through Hungary to Germany and hence to England, when George I became king. Both his mother and his wife bore this name. Sophie is the anglicized form which was very popular in the 18th century. The form **Sophy** is also used.

SORCHA see SARAH

SPENCER m. (spen'_se)

The earlier form of this name was **Spenser**, a surname which was a contraction of 'dispenser', an administrator of supplies in feudal times. The Le Despenser family came to power under Henry III, and by the 17th century the name had become Spencer, which was the form Sir Winston Churchill inherited. The name is also found in North America where the actor Spencer Tracy (1900-67) gave it fame.

STACEY, STACY m. and f. (stā′sē)

a pet form which has become popular as an independent name. For men it was a short form of EUSTACE; as a woman's name it was originally short for ANASTASIA.

STANLEY m. (stan′li)

This was originally a surname derived from an old Anglo-Saxon place name meaning 'stony field', and hence probably meant a person from such a place. It was first used as a first name in the mid-19th century, because of its aristocratic connotation. The name later became popular in imitation of the explorer John Rowlands, who adopted Stanley as a pseudonym. His fame led to its rapid spread. It has the short form **Stan**.

STEF(F)AN see STEPHEN

STELLA f. (stel′e)

This is the Latin word for 'star'. The earliest use of this name was by Roman Catholics, Stella Maris, meaning Star of the Sea, being a title of invocation of the Virgin Mary. The more general use of the name in modern times is due to its literary associations. An early literary use was in Sir Philip Sidney's *Astrophel and Stella* (1591). In the early 18th century Jonathan Swift used it as a pet name in various poems to Esther Johnson. Other forms are ESTELLA and **Estelle**, the former being used by Dickens in his novel *Great Expectations* (1861).

STEPHANIE *f.* (stef'*eni*)

This is the French feminine form derived from the Latin **Stephanus** (*see* STEPHEN). It is frequently used in Britain.

STEPHEN, STEVEN *m.* (ste'*ven*)

from the Greek **Stephanos**, meaning 'crown' or 'wreath'. The laurel wreath was the highest honour a man could attain in the classical world. Stephen was a common personal name in Ancient Greece, and it was borne by the very first Christian martyr, Stephen the Deacon (Acts VI & VII). The name is first recorded in this country in Domesday Book in the Latin form **Stephan(us)**. After the Norman Conquest its popularity increased. **Steve** and **Stevie** are the modern pet forms. There is also a Welsh form, **Steffan**, and the Continental **Stefan** is also used.

STEWART *see* STUART

ST JOHN *m. (sin'jn)*

the name of the saint, used as a first name. Charlotte Bronte has a character of this name in *Jane Eyre* (1847). The politican Norman St John Stevas, now Lord St John, is a well-known user of the name.

STUART *m. (stū'et)*

from the Old English *sti weard*, an official who looked after the animals kept for food. Though it has changed its meaning somewhat, it survives as 'steward' today. The man who founded the Royal House of Scotland in the 14th century was Walter the High Steward. Because of this, and the romantic associations of the name with the Jacobite cause in the 18th century, Stuart and the alternative **Stewart**, are now common as surnames and as first names. **Stuert** is also used.

SUSAN, SUSANNA(H) *f. (soo'zen, soozan'e)*

Shushannah is Hebrew for 'lily' and Susanna(h) was the earliest form of this name in England, occuring in the Middle Ages and becoming quite common after the

Reformation. Susan was adopted in the 18th century and superseded the earliest form completely in the 19th century. In the 20th century the French **Suzanne** and **Suzette** have also been used in Britain. **Sue, Sukey, Susie** and **Suzy** are common short forms.

SYBIL *see* **SIBYL**

SYDNEY *see* **SIDNEY**

SYLVESTER, SYLVESTRA *see* **SILVESTER**

SYLVIA *see* **SILVIA**

T

TABITHA *f.* (*tab'ithe*)

from the Aramaic, meaning 'gazelle'. In the New Testament (Acts IX) it is the name of a Christian woman of Joppa, who showed great charity towards the poor (*see* DORCAS). **Tabatha** is a modern spelling of the name.

TADHGH *see* **TIMOTHY**

TAFFY *see* **DAVID**

TALITHA *f.* (*talith'e*)

from an Aramaic word meaning 'girl'. It has very occasionally been used in the 20th century.

TALMAI *see* **BARTHOLEMEW**

TAM *see* **THOMAS**

TAMARA f. (*temà're*)

Tamara is the Russian form of the Biblical name **Tamar**, which means 'date palm'. Tamara was the name of a famous Russian queen, and remains a popular name in Russia. In the West Country Tamar (*ĭmà r*) can come from the river that separats Devon from Cornwall.

TAMMY f. (*tam'e*)

a pet form of TAMARA, TAMSIN and THOMASINE, now used as an independent name. In 1957 a film *Tammy* and a song which was a number one hit in the US for three weeks started a vogue for the name's use.

TAMASINE, TAMSIN see THOMASIN

TANCRED m. (*tank'red*)

from the Old German meaning 'think counsel'. Tancred was the Norman form, which has occasionally been used in England since the Conquest.

TANIA, TANYA see TATIANA

TANITH f. (tan'ith)

Tha name of a Phoenician goddess of love, that has recently come into occasional use as a first name. It can also take the form **Tanit**.

TANSY f. (tan'ze)

The name of a yellow wild flower used as a first name. It can also be a pet form of ANASTASIA.

TARA f. (tà're)

Tara is the name of the hill where the ancient High Kings of Ireland held court. It plays an important part in Irish legend. It has only been used as a first name this century.

TATIANA f. (tatià'ne)

This name has been popular in Russia for a long time, especially in its abbreviated forms **Tania**, **Tanya** and **Tonya** which are sometimes used in Britain. There were several saints named Tatianus, the masculine form, and a St Tatiana, a martyr of the Greek Orthodox Church.

TEBALD, TIBALD, TYBALT see THEOBALD

TED, TEDDY *see* EDMOND, EDWARD, THEODORE

TEDDY *see* THEODORE

TERENCE *m.* (ter'ens)

from the Latin Terentius, the name of a famous Roman comic playwright. Short forms are **Terry** and **Tel**. It is now also found in the forms **Ter(r)ance** and **Terrell**. It has only recently been used in this country having come from Ireland, where it is used to transliterate the native **Turlough**, meaning 'like Thor' the Norse thunder god (*see also* THEODORIC).

TERESA, THERESA *f.* (terā′ze, terēse)

It has been suggested that this name was originally spelt **Therasia**, which was the name of two Greek islands, and so meant a woman from that place. Otherwise its derivation is obscure. The first recorded Therasia was the wife of the 5th century St Paulinus, and was responsible for his conversion. The name was for a long time confined to Spain, where it flourished until the 16th century. After this, St Teresa of Avila spread the name to all Roman Catholic countries, but it did not become common in this country until the 18th century. It is often abbreviated to **Tess**, **Tessa** or **Tessie**. The form **Terry**, shared with other, masculine names, is also found. A variant is TRAC(E)Y.

TERRY *see* **TERENCE, TERESA, THEODORIC**

TESS, TESSA, TESSIE *see* **TERESA**

TEWDWR *see* **THEODORE**

THEA *see* **DOROTHEA, THEODORA**

THELMA *f.* (*thel'me*)

Like MAVIS, this name was invented in the 19th century by the writer Marie Corelli, in her novel *Thelma* (1887), and spread quickly throughout the country. There is a Greek word *thelma*, meaning 'will', which may have had some influence on its development.

THEO *see* **THEOBALD, THEODORA, THEODORE**

THEOBALD *m.* (*thē'ebawld*)

from the Old German **Theudobald**, meaning 'people bold'. Theobeald was the Anglo-Saxon form which was reinforced at the Conquest by the Norman Theobald. This settled down as **Tebald**, **Tibald** and **Tybalt**, but remained Theobaldus in Latin documents. The use of Tibs, Tibbles and Tibbie as a name for a cat comes from the medieval animal story *Reynard the Fox*, in which the cunning cat is called **Tybalt**. The abbreviation **Theo** is shared with other names having this stem.

THEODORA f. (thēedaw're)

This is the feminine form of THEODORE, which has been used since the 17th century. It is usually abbreviated to **Theo**, **Thea** and **Dora** (*see* DOROTHEA).

THEODORE m. (thē'edaw)

from the Greek, meaning 'gift of God'. There are 28 saints of this name in the Church Calendar. In England the name did not become general until the 19th century, but in Wales it has long had the form **Tewdwr** or **Tudor**, the name of the dynasty founded by Henry VII. The usual abbreviation in North America is **Teddy**, and the now universal teddy bear was thus named because of President Theodore Roosevelt's passion for big-game hunting. In

England **Theo** is a more common abbreviation.

THEODORIC m. (thēod'erik)

from the Old German, meaning 'people's ruler'. The Old English form of the name was Theodric which in medieval times became **Terry**, and in French **Thierry**. Theodoric became the most common form in the 18th century, but it is rare in Britain today (*see* DEREK).

THEODOSIA f. (thēodō'sie)

from the Greek, meaning 'god-given'. It has been used occasionally in Britain since the 17th century.

THEODRIC *see* **THEODORIC**

THEOPHANIA *see* **TIFFANY**

THERASIA, THERESIA *see* **TERESA**

THERESA *see* **TERESA**

THEUDOBALD *see* **THEOBALD**

THOMAS *m.* (*tom'es*)

from the Aramaic, meaning 'twin'. It was first given by Jesus to an Apostle named Judas, to distinguish him from Judas Iscariot and Jude. In England it occurs only as a priest's name until the Norman Conquest, after which it became common. The abbreviation **Tom** appears in the Middle Ages. **Tam** and **Tammy** are the Scottish pet forms. The use of **Tommy** as a nickname for a British private soldier goes back to the 19th century, when the enlistment form had on it the specimen signature 'Thomas Atkins'.

THOMASIN(E) *f.* (*tom'esin*)

These are feminine diminutives of THOMAS. They have been used since the Middle Ages. **Tamasine** and **Tamsin** are West Country variants and there has been some revival of the latter in recent years. **Thomasina** is an old latinized version which was revived in the 19th century. TAMMY is a short form.

THOR *see* THURSTAN

THORA f. (thaw're)

from the Norse, meaning 'dedicated to Thor'.
Thor was the god of thunder in Norse mythology, and he also gave his name to 'Thursday'.
Thora is a rare name in Britain, but well
known from the actress Thora Hird.

THORKETILL see TORQUIL

THURSTAN m. (the'sten)

From the Norse, meaning 'Thor stone', Thor
was one of the principal Old Norse gods, and
his name means 'thunder'. The Danes brought
the name to England before the Norman Conquest and it has been in use ever since, though
it is now rare.

TIBBIE, TIBBLES, TIBS see THEOBALD

TIFFANY f. (tif'enē)

was originally a pet form of the name Theophania, from the Greek meaning 'the mani-
festation of God' Tifaine was the Old French
form, and this name was given to girls born at
the time of Epiphany, the words having the
same meaning. These names were rare until

recently, but Tiffany is now a very popular name.

TILLY *see* MATILDA

TIMOTHY *m.* (*tim'ethi*)

Timotheos is an old Greek name meaning 'honouring God'. Its use as a Christian name is due to Timothy, the companion of St Paul. It was not used anywhere in Europe until the 16th century, when many classical and biblical names were revived. **Tim** and **Timmy** are the abbreviations. In Ireland Timothy has for a long time been used as an equivalent for the native **Tadhgh** which means 'poet'. It is one of the commonest boys' names in Britain today. **Timothea** is a rare feminine form.

TINA *f.* (*tē'ne*)

originally a short form of girls' names ending in '-tina', commonest of which is CHRISTINA. It is now used as a name in its own right.

TITUS *m.* (*tit'es*)

This is a Latin name of unknown meaning. Two well-known holders of the name were a

349

follower of St Paul, and in contrast, the infamous Titus Oates, an English conspirator and perjurer of the 17th century. It is probably best known today as the name of the hero of Mervyn Peake's *Gormenghast* books.

TOBIAS, TOBY *m.* (*tōbi′es, tō′bi*)

These are respectively the Greek and English forms of an Old Hebrew name which means 'the Lord is good'. The story of 'Tobias and the Angel', which is told in the Book of Tobit in the Apocrypha, was a favourite one in the Middle Ages. Punch's dog Toby is named after the dog that accompanied Tobias on his travels. The 'Toby jug' is probably thus named in honour of a fictional 18th-century drinker, Toby Philpot.

TOD(D) *m.* (*tod*)

A surname, meaning 'fox', which has now come to be used as a first name.

TOINETTE *see* ANTONY

TOM, TOMMY *see* THOMAS

TONI, TONY *see* ANTONY

TORCULL *see* **TORQUIL**

TORIA *see* **VICTORIA**

TORMOD *see* **NORMAN**

TORQUIL *m. (tawk'wil)*

This is the English rendering of the Norse name, Thorketill, 'Thor's cauldron'. The first element is the name of the Norse thunder God Thor. The original became **Torcull** in Gaelic, which was anglicized into Torquil. It is used in Scotland, especially in the Outer Hebrides and among the Macleod family, and it has occasionally been given in England.

TOTTY *see* **CHARLOTTE**

TRAC(E)Y *f. and m. (trā'sē)*

This popular girl's name seems to have started life as a pet form of TERESA. Its use as an independent name was probably helped by the use of the surname (from a French place name) as a boy's name; particularly as at the time when it first became popular Spencer Tracy (1900-67) was a well-known film star.

TRAVIS *m.* (*tra'vis*)

A surname used as a first name. It comes from the French word meaning 'crossroads', which may have been given to a toll-collector.

TREVOR *m.* (*trev'e*)

from the Welsh **Trefor**, meaning 'great homestead'. Trevor is the English spelling of this.

TRICIA *see* PATRICIA

TRISTRAM, TRISTAN *m.* (*tris'trem*)

from the Celtic Dryustan, meaning 'tumult' or 'din'. Tristram occurs from the 12th century only, and it soon became confused with the French Tristan, derived from *triste*, meaning 'sad'. It is known for the novel *Tristram Shandy* (1759-67) by Lawrence Sterne and as the name of the hero of the great medieval story of doomed love *Tristan and Isolde*. **Tristran** is also found.

TRIXIE *see* BEATRICE

TROY *m.* (*troē*)

Troy was the ancient city in Asia Minor besieged by the Greeks for ten years in order to win back the beautiful Helen for her husband. Its use as a first name was boosted in the 1950s by the actor Troy Donohue.

TRUDIE *see* **GERTRUDE**

TUDOR *see* **THEODORE**

TURLOUGH *see* **TERENCE**

TYRONE *m.* (*tīrō′n*)

The name of the Irish county, which means 'Owen's county', used as a first name. It was used in the past by the actor Tyrone Power (1913-58) in the US and by the British theatre director Sir Tyrone Guthrie (1900-71). **Ty** is the short form, although Guthrie was known to his friends as Tony.

U

ULICK *see* **ULYSSES**

ULYSSES *m.* (*ū'lisēs*)

This is the Latin name for the Greek hero **Odysseus**, whose tale is told in Homer's *Odyssey*. Though little used in England, Scotland or Wales, it has often been used in Ireland as an equivalent for the Irish **Ulick**, meaning 'mind reward'. In 1922 James Joyce's famous novel *Ulysses* was published.

UMBERTO *see* **HUMBERT**

UNA *f.* (*óó'ne, ū'ne*)

The etymology of this ancient Irish name is obscure. The true Irish spelling of the name is **Oonagh** or **Oona**, both of which are also found in Scotland. **Juno**, from the influence of the name of the Roman queen of the gods, is another Irish form, best known for Sean O'Casey's play *Juno and the Paycock* (1924).

The Elizabethan poet Edmund Spenser took the Irish name Una and gave it its Latin sense, 'one unity', in his epic poem *The Faerie Queene*.

UNITY *f.* (*ūˈniti*)

This is one of the abstract virtue names that became quite common among Puritans after the Reformation. It is only rarely found today.

URSULA *f.* (*esˈūle*)

from the Latin, meaning 'little she-bear'. The name was fairly common in the Middle Ages on account of St Ursula, a 5th-century Cornish princess, who, with her companions, was killed by hostile inhabitants when shipwrecked near Cologne. The name had a revival when the novel *John Halifax, Gentleman* (1856), by Mrs Craik, became popular, in which the heroine's name was Ursula. The actress Ursula Andress (b.1936) is probably the best known modern user.

V

VAL *see* **VALERIE**

VALENTINE *m. and f. (val'entīn)*

from Latin *valens*, meaning 'strong', or
'healthy'. St Valentine was a 3rd-century
Roman priest whose martyrdom happened to
fall on February 14th, the eve of the cel-
ebrations of the pagan goddess Juno, when
lots were drawn to choose lovers. The pagan
festival was absorbed by the Christian religion
and is still celebrated today. The custom of
sending cards was started in the 19th century.
The name has been used in Britain since the
13th century and can be used for either sex.
Valentina is an alternative feminine form.
Val is a common diminutive, shared with
Valerie.

VALERIE *f. (vel'eri)*

Valérie was the French form of the Roman
family name **Valeria**, and was taken into use

in Britain in the late 19th century. It comes from the verb 'to be in good health'. It has the short form Val.

VANDA *see* **WANDA**

VANESSA *f.* (*venes'e*)

This name was invented in the early 18th century by the poet Jonathan Swift as a pet name for Esther Vanhomrigh. He took the first syllable of her surname and added Essa, which was a pet form of Esther.

VARIN *see* **WARREN**

VAUGHN, VAUGHAN *m.* (*vawn*)

from the Welsh **Vychan**, meaning 'small one'. It is mainly used in the United States.

VELMA *f.* (*vel'me*)

a name of unknown origin, which came into use in the 1880s in the United States.

VENETIA *f.* (*venēsh'ie*)

the Latin for the Italian city of Venice used as a first name. In the past the name was thought to have some connection with **Venus**, the Roman goddess of love.

VERA f. (vēr'e)

This name has two possible derivations. One possible source is the Russian for 'faith', another is the Latin meaning 'true'. It was used in English literature in the 19th century, and became popular in Britain at the beginning of the 20th. It is sometimes used as an abbreviation of VERONICA. **Verena** is an alternative form of the name.

VERILY see VERITY

VERITY f. (ver'iti)

from the English word for 'truth'. It was first used by the Puritans in the 17th century, and has been quite common ever since. The variant, **Verily**, is also found occasionally.

VERNA f. (ve'ne)

This is a Latin word meaning 'spring-like' and it is occasionally used as a Christian name in Britain today.

VERNON *m.* (*ver'nen*)

Richard de Vernon was one of the companions of William the Conqueror. The surname derives from a French place name which means 'little alder grove'. It was not used as a Christian name until the 19th century, when many such aristocratic names were taken into general use.

VERONICA *f.* (*veron'ike*)

from Latin *vera iconica*, meaning 'a true image'. St Veronica is the name given by tradition to the woman who wiped Christ's face when he was on his way to Calvary. A 'true image' of Christ's face was supposed to have appeared on the piece of rag she used. **Véronique** has long been popular in France, and it was from there that the name reached Scotland in the late 17th century. It does not appear much in England before the late 19th century, but is now fairly common. H.G. Wells' novel *Ann Veronica* (1909) may have contributed to its popularity.

VIC *see* **VICTOR**

VICKIE, VICKY, VIKKI *see* **VICTORIA**

VICTOR m. (*vik'te*)

This is Latin for 'conqueror'. Although it occurs in medieval England it was not common until the 19th century, when Victor was used as a masculine equivalent of VICTORIA and became very common. The common short form is **Vic**.

VICTORIA f. (*viktaw'rie*)

from the Latin meaning 'victory'. This name was hardly used in this country until the reign of Queen Victoria, who was named after her mother. The name has never been particularly fashionable, and today is more often found in one of its short forms, **Vick(y)**, **Vickie**, **Vikki** and **Toria**. **Vita** and **Viti** and the pet name **Queenie** are also found.

VILMA see WILLIAM

VINCENT m. (*vin'sent*)

from the Latin, meaning 'conquering'. There was a 3rd-century Spanish martyr of this name whose cult was widespread. The name occurs in English records from the 13th century and gave rise to the surnames Vincent, Vincey and Vince. It was, however, the 17th-century St Vincent de Paul who caused the name to be revived. He founded the Vincentian Order of the Sisters of Charity. The name became quite common in the 19th century, and the usual short form is **Vince**.

VIOLA, VIOLET f. (vī'ole, vī'olet)

Viola is Latin for 'violet'. Although it does occur in the Middle Ages, the modern use of this name is due to Shakespeare, who gave it to the heroine of *Twelfth Night* (1600). It has never been as common as Violet. **Violette** and **Violetta** have also been used.

VIRGIL m. (ve'jil)

the name of a great Roman poet. The American composer Virgil Thomson (b.1896) is a famous modern example of the name.

VIRGINIA f. (vejin'ie)

Although there was a Roman family called Virginus, the modern use of this name dates only from 1584, when Sir Walter Raleigh called his newly founded colony in North America, Virginia, after Elizabeth Tudor, the 'Virgin Queen'. **Ginny** is a common pet form.

VITA, VITI see VICTORIA

VITUS *see* **GUY**

VIVIAN, VIVIEN *m. and f.* (*viv′ēen*)

comes from the Latin **Vivianus**, which means 'lively'. Vivian is now used for both sexes, but was originally the masculine form, with Vivien for the feminine, from the French **Vivienne**. Forms such as **Vyvian** are also found, and **Viv** is used for short.

W

WAL, WALLY *see* **WALLACE, WALTER**

WALDHAR *see* **WALTER**

WALLACE *m.* (*wol'es*)

from the surname of Sir William Wallace, the
great Scottish patriot of the 13th century. The
use of his name as a Christian name started
about a hundred years ago. The name is
derived from the Old English meaning
'foreign'. Another spelling of the name is
Wallis, and this form is popular in North
America where it is used for both sexes. The
short forms **Wal** and **Wally** are shared with
Walter.

WALTER *m.* (*wawl'te*)

from the Old German Waldhar, meaning 'rule
people'. Walter was very popular among the
Normans, and the name quickly became established in England. Sir Walter Raleigh is a

well-known historical example; he used the short form **Wat** for his son. **Walt**, **Wal** and **Wallis** are more popular short forms today, and Walt is used as a separate name in North America.

WANDA f. *(won'de)*

This is a German feminine name probably connected with the word 'vandal'. Its use in this country is recent, possibly starting when a novel of that name by Ouida was published in 1883. **Vanda** and **Vonda** are variants.

WARNER m. *(waw'ne)*

from the Old German, meaning 'Varin folk'. The Normans introduced the name to England as **Garnier**, which gave us the surnames Garner and Warner. It is largely through taking the surname as a first name that Warner has been used in modern times. It is particularly popular in North America.

WARREN m. *(wor'en)*

from the Old German folk-name **Varin**, which may mean 'defender'. The Normans introduced the forms **Warin** and **Guarin** to England and these led to the surnames Warren, Waring and Garnet.

WARWICK m. (wo'rik)

the name of the English town, which means 'houses by the weir', used as a first name. **Warrie** is used as a pet form.

WAYNE m. (wān)

This is a surname meaning 'cart' or 'cartmaker'. Its use as a first name is mainly due to the great popularity of the actor John Wayne (1907-79).

WENDY f. (wen'di)

This name was first used by James Barrie in *Peter Pan* (1904). The name started as 'Friendly-Wendy' a pet name for Barrie used by a child friend of his, Margaret Henley. The name has become quite common since.

WESLEY m. (wez'lē)

John and Charles Wesley were the founders of Methodism, and the name came to be used as a first name in their honour. As a surname it means 'west meadow'. *Wes* is a short form.

WIDO see **GUY**

WILBUR m. (wil'be)

This name is very popular in North America but is practically unknown in Britain. It has been suggested that it originated with Dutch settlers in America, and may come from Wildeboer, the Dutch for 'wild farmer'. Another possible source is the Old German Williburg, meaning 'resolute protection'. The most famous example was Wilbur Wright, who, with his brother Orville, made the first successful powered flight in 1903.

WILFRED, WILFRID m. (wil'frid)

from the Old English **Wilfrith**, meaning 'will peace'. St Wilfrid was an important figure in the 7th century, and his name was particularly popular in Yorkshire, where he preached and founded the sees of Ripon and Hexham. The name did not survive the Norman Conquest but was revived by the high church Anglicans in the 19th century. It has the pet form **Wilf**.

WILLIAM, WILMA m. (wil'iem, wil'me)

from the Old German, meaning 'will helmet'. William was always a popular name with the

Normans, who brought it to England, and, until the 13th century when it was ousted by John, it was the commonest of all names in England. **Will** or **Willie** are the old short forms but **Bill** and **Billie** are more usual today. **Gwilym** is the Welsh form of the name, and **Liam** a short form which has spread from Ireland. Feminine forms which have been used occasionally are **Wilhelmina** and Wilma, and short forms include **Willa** or **Vilma**, **Minnie** and **Minna**. These feminine forms are more popular in America where German immigrants have spread their use.

WINIFRED *f.* (*win'ifrid*)

from the Welsh feminine name **Gwenfrewi**, anglicized as Winifred and later confused with the Old English male name **Winfrith**, meaning 'friend of peace'. St Winifred, a 7th-century saint, was killed by Caradog, a chieftain from Hawarden in Flintshire. Although she was a popular saint in the Middle Ages, her name was not really used much until the 16th century. **Win**, **Winnie** and less often **Freda**, are short forms. **Winifrid** is also used.

WINSTON *m.* (*win'sten*)

This is the name of a small village in Gloucestershire, and probably means 'friend's settlement'. The name has been used in the Churchill family since 1620, when Sir Winston Churchill, father of the 1st Duke of Marlborough, was born. His mother was Sarah Winston. During the last World War, the second Sir Winston Churchill became famous, and the name has since become more widely used in his honour.

WYNDHAM *m.* (*win'dem*)

from the Old English Windham, meaning 'from the enclosure with the winding path'. It is not a common name.

WYN, WYNNE *see* GWYN

X

XANTHE f. (*zan'thi*)

from the Greek meaning 'yellow'. It has occasionally been used in Britain.

XAVIER m. (*zav'ēe*)

the surname of St Francis Xavier (1506-52) used as a first name. It is occasionally spelt **Zavier**, and there are rare feminine forms, **Xavia**, **Zavia** and **Xaverine**.

XENIA f. (*zen'ie*)

from the Greek, meaning 'hospitable one'. It is only occasionally found.

Y

YASMIN(E) *see* **JASMINE**

YEHUDI *see* **JUDE**

YOLANDA *f.* (*yoland'i*)

from the Greek, meaning 'violet flower'. The
Gilbert and Sullivan *Iolanthe* comes from the
same root. **Yolande** is the French form.

YVES *see* **IVOR, YVONNE**

YVONNE, YVETTE *f.* (*ēvon', ēvet'*)

from the Old French, meaning 'yew bow'. It is
the feminine diminutive of the common Breton
name **Yves**. The masculine name has never
been common in Britain, but the feminine
forms are quite popular.

Z

ZACCHAEUS *m.* (*zakē'es*)

This is a latinization of the Hebrew **Zakkai**, an abbreviation of Zachariah (*see* ZACHARIAS). In the New Testament (Luke XIX) Zacchaeus was the name of the publican who climbed into a tree to get a better view when Jesus passed by, and later entertained him at his house. The name was much used by Puritans in the 17th century but is now obsolete.

ZACHARIAS, ZACHARY *m.* (*zakerī'es, zak'eri*)

These are respectively the Greek and English forms of the Hebrew **Zachariah** or **Zechariah**, meaning 'the Lord has remembered'. Zachary was used occasionally in the Middle Ages, but did not become at all common until the Puritans adopted it in the 17th century. They took it to America where it has recently become very popular, together with the short form **Zak**.

ZAK *see* **ZACHARIAS, ISAAC**

ZAKKAI *see* **ZACCHAEUS**

ZANDRA *see* **SANDRA**

ZARA *f.* (*zà're*)

is an Arabic name meaning 'brightness, splendour of dawn'. It has a long history of literary use, but came to the attention of the general public in 1981 when the Princess Royal used it as her daughter's name.

ZAVIA, ZAVIER *see* **XAVIER**

ZEKE *see* **EZEKIEL**

ZELDA *see* **GRISELDA**

ZENA *f.* (*ze'ne*)

This name comes from a Persian word meaning 'woman'.

ZENOBIA *f.* (*zenō'bie*)

This was the name of a great Queen of Palmyra in modern Syria in the 3rd century AD. She ruled the Eastern Roman Empire, and her aggressive foreign policy made it necessary for the Emperor Aurelian to wage war on her. This he did successfully, and put an end to her power, though he spared her life. The name occurs in Cornwall from the 16th century but the reason for this is unknown.

ZILLAH f. (zil'e)

from the Hebrew for 'shade'. The name occurs in the Old Testament (Genesis IV, 19-23), and was used occasionally after the Reformation. Today it survives particularly among gypsies.

ZOE f. (zō'ē)

This is the Greek word for 'life'. The Alexandrian Jews used it to translate the Hebrew equivalent for Eve into Greek, Eve being the 'mother of life'. The name spread throughout the Eastern Church but has only been used in Britain in the last hundred years. It is now very popular.

ZOLA f. (zō'le)

the name of the French novelist Emile Zola (1840-1902) used as a first name. Although best known from the runner Zola Budd, the name has been used before. The lead singer of the 1950s pop group The Platters was Zola Taylor.

ZULEIKA *f.* (*ziŏŏlī'ke̲*, *ziŏŏlē'ke̲*)

from the Persian, meaning 'brilliant beauty'. The name is known from Max Beerbohm's satirical novel *Zuleika Dobson* (1911), whose heroine is so beautiful that all the young men at Oxford University kill themselves for love of her.